A Fresh Look at
Biblical Events

Gene W. Money

Contents

Four Friends

Mark 2: 1-12

"Sari! Oh Sari. Are you home?"

The woman peered into the window of the small house. It was dusk and getting rather dark inside and she saw that there was no lamp burning.

"Well," she thought, "where could they be? I have seen neither hide nor hair of them all day. I wonder if something is wrong."

Just as she had decided that there was no one there her neighbor came around the house carrying a pot of water.

"Greetings Joanna, I thought that it was you that I heard. Come on in. I was just about to fix us something to eat. We have been gone all day and the fire is out. I guess it will have to be just cold mutton and bread for tonight. Maybe with a little sweet wine."

As Sari lit a lamp and began to get out some bowls, Joanna said, "Where in the world have you been all day. I was here early and you were already gone. Is something wrong? Where is Joash? Is he not home yet?"

Sari laughed and replied, "I can see that you are just eaten up with curiosity so I suppose that I will have to just sit down and tell you the whole story. Of course, I was going to in the morning anyway. And Joash stopped down the way to talk with the rabbi. He will be along in a bit."

Joanna took a seat on the bench near the door and said, "Whatever is going on with you I think you must be happy about, from the look on your face."

"You are right about that. Joash and I are very happy, and I think that Tamar is happy too."

Joanna sprang to her feet and exclaimed, "Oh, now I know. You have made an arrangement for Tamar to get married. I would think that it is that young fellow who lives over behind your mother's house. Is that right?"

Still with a smile on her face Sari said, "No, you are wrong. She will be marrying a young man from over at Capernaum. His name is Perez and he comes from a very good family. Since Tamar has gotten to be of marriageable age she has been rather concerned about who we might find for her. Of course we all were at that age, but she is very pleased about Perez.

"Perez, you say? The only Perez I know of over at Capernaum is that man that got hurt when he was run over by a wild donkey. The last I heard he was paralyzed, and they say there is no hope of him getting any better. It surely must be someone else."

"No, it is him. The very one. He is as good as he was before the accident."

"Sari, my husband saw that boy about a year ago and he told me that Perez could not even stand, much less take a step. They must have a good doctor in Capernaum or perhaps a miracle worker. They said that he has to be carried

5

everywhere he goes. Are you sure we are talking about the same person?"

"I am sure that he is the one and you have just said how he was cured. Joanna, there is a miracle worker in Capernaum. You just sit back down and I will tell you how it happened, and we got it straight from Perez himself. "

The boy was almost eighteen years old when he began to work with his father and uncles, hauling freight to and from the ocean port at Caesarea. It had always been hard work wrestling balky donkeys over the rough roads, particularly through the hill country South of Mt. Carmel. Difficult or not, Perez loved being part of the family business. Even on the two occasions when robbers had attempted to steal part of their cargo, Perez was exhilarated and spent hours recounted the experiences. Yet, his very enthusiasm for the work may have played a part in his injury.

Perez and one of his uncles were just leaving Capernaum with seven animals loaded with wine from the vineyards in the Jordan Valley when one of the donkeys, young and just broken, began to buck and run. Perez dropped the line with which had been leading the lead burro. He ran after the fleeing animal, grabbing it by the halter and holding on with all his might. Perez was dragged along for several yards before the donkey plunged into a deep ravine, tumbling over and over and then coming to rest with the animal on top of the boy. The donkey was not badly hurt and, in its efforts, to get to its feet it badly mauled the young man who was already unconscious from the fall into the rocky ravine.

It was some minutes before help arrived and he was carried to a nearby house. It was soon apparent that he was badly hurt. Perez was unable to move his legs and his arms were restricted in movement.

Weeks and months passed and so did the hope that he would ever get any better. Perez at last suggested that he be placed on the main road in front of the synagogue so that he could beg there, thinking that he would be less of a burden to his family. But the family would not hear of it. They proclaimed that they would take care of their own.

Perez had an older brother named Josiah who spent a lot of time taking care of him. It was the talk of the town how one brother was so concerned and caring of the younger one. Not only did Josiah care, he decided to do something about it. He had heard of a traveling teacher who was said to work miracles of healing. The man, called Jesus, spent a lot of time in Capernaum and Josiah had heard him teach and seen him lay his hands on a blind man and heal him. Josiah became a believer in the teacher's message and in his ability to restore the sick to health. So a resolve was born to get Perez to see the man, Jesus.

It was not long before the word came that the teacher was in town and was residing in a house about one half mile from where the brothers lived. Josiah called on three of his friends to help and they decided that they would get Perez over to see the teacher early the next morning before many people were there. Josiah knew that the teacher was drawing crowds but he figured that being there shortly after sun—up would be the best time.

With one man on each corner of the litter they set off on their mission. The three friends were rather skeptical that anything could be done for the boy but they agreed that nothing else had done any good so why not try one more thing.

As they hurried along the dusty road that early morning Josiah told his brother not to worry, things were looking up. "I have great faith in this man, Jesus," he said. "Would I call on my friends to work this hard if I had any doubts?"

As the quartet of litter bearers topped the hill just before arriving at their destination they were astounded to see what looked like most of the towns people gathered around the house. In fact, they could not even see the front door for the throng.

"What are we going to do Josiah?" one of the group said. "We won't be able to get near the teacher."

"Sure we will," Josiah replied. When they see who we have here and what shape he is in they will make way for us.

But it was not to be. When the four approached the house with their burden people began to say, "You can wait your turn. We have been here since before first light." One old woman said, "What do you want to bring that boy here for? The master is teaching today. He will not be bothered by someone in that bad a shape. Everybody knows that the boy will never get up again." The four set the stretcher down in the shade of an olive tree and began to talk about what should be their next move. The three friends had caught the spirit of faith that Josiah had and were unwilling to give up in face of this difficulty.

First off they decided that they would not just wait until the crowd dispersed. There was just no telling when that would happen. They knew that they were going to do something right now. But what?

"Look, the house has the low flat roof just like our house. Remember how father fell through the roof one time when he was repairing it. Wouldn't it be easy to just open up a hole and take some ropes and let Perez right down into the room with the teacher?"

This idea by Josiah brought a smile to Perez. Just the daring of it appealed to him. "That's a great plan Josiah. You will not have to worry about dropping me. What more damage could be done?"

One of them spoke up. "Let's go around back and go right up the back stairs. Then I will run and get some rope. I know where I can get some."

Arriving at the back of the house they were downcast to discover that there was no outside stairs to the roof of the house. Now what?

Even Josiah was nonplused. It looked as if they stumped but then Perez spoke up, "Look around the corner of the next house and see if they don't have an outside stairway. See, the two houses are only three or four paces apart. If we can get on top of the other house, we can get over to the roof of this one."

"I think you have something there Perez. While I get the rope one of you run down to the carpenter's shop and borrow some long poles."

While two of Josiah's helpers went for the equipment he and the other helper carried the stretcher around to the foot of the stairs of the neighboring house. In a few minutes the two returned with the needed rope and poles and one of them took them to the roof top.

"What do you think?" Josiah asked. "Should we build the bridge across first, or should we take Perez up there first?"

"I want to go up now and watch you put in the poles. I may have a suggestion or two about how to do it."

Going up the stairs was a bit harder than carrying the man along on the ground. There was much grunting and yelled warning to be careful on the stairs that were not built to hold all that weight at one time. The noise soon brought and old woman out to see what was going on.

"What are doing up on my roof. And what are you doing with all that stuff. Come down right now. It's bad enough to have a whole mob of people in the street stirring up all that dust but now I have you on my roof too. I would go get my husband right now if he wasn't over there in that crowd at the neighbors."

Josiah leaned out over the edge of the roof. "Hello Mariam, don 't you know us? It's Josiah and Perez and some friends and we are here to help Perez get to the teacher so he can be healed. I knew that you would not mind if we used your house."

"Yes Josiah, I know you, but how is being on my house going to help that boy?"

"Just you watch. We have it all figured out."

Mariam watched as the young men laid the four poles across from one roof to the other. Then they were tied together with stout cord. After one of them made an experimental crossing to see if would hold together they decided it was time to do the deed.

This time each end of the litter would have to carried by just one person, but they decided it would better that way because the load would be lighter. With Josiah on one end and the lighter of the friends on the other they started the slow trip across. About half way across the poles began to bend and one of them made a cracking noise but they were afraid to stop. In as little time as it takes to tell it they had

Perez on the roof of the house where the teacher and healer was talking.

They were all grinning and laughing as they realized they could breathe now. They had made it.

"Now let's get the roof opened. Two of us can do that while the other two get the ropes tied to the corners of the stretcher."

When the dust began to fall of the heads of multitude that had gotten into the house there was some consternation to say the least. The master of the house yelled out to window and asked, or rather demanded that someone see what was going on up on the roof. But Jesus held up a hand and said, "Let them be. I think that something good is going on here.

The crowd moved back against the wall as best they could and watched as the hole in the ceiling grew larger. Then watched in amazement as the litter was slowly lowered into the room. Jesus looked at the four peering down through the opening and then to the young man lying on the litter.

The crowd was hushed in expectation of what the teacher was going to say to them. In a kind voice Jesus, looking at Perez, said, "Son, your sins are forgiven." There was a murmur that went through the crowd about how a man can forgive sins. Jesus perceiving their thoughts said, "Which is easier, to forgive sins or to heal a paralytic? To show that I have the power to do both (turning to Perez lying on the stretcher) get up, take your mat and go home."

Perez sprang to his feet and the crowd parted like the Red Sea as he carried his stretcher from the of friends still on the roof.

"That's the story. Just like Perez told going to be my son-in-law. What do you think of that, dear?"

Perez

"Perez, I just don't know why you have to go all the way to Judaea right now. You know that I am almost in a family way and your uncle says he will be needing all the help he can get with that shipment of oil from Caesarea.

The couple stood facing each other across the front room of their modest house. They were young, barely into their twenties. He was tall and muscular, looking very able to handle the donkeys and heavy freight that he and an uncle moved from the sea to their town of Capernaum. He, Perez, had been badly hurt in an accident a few years before but had been cured by the teacher and healer, Jesus, who had spent many days in their city.

Tamar, Perez 's wife, looked even younger than he and now wore an anxious and angry expression on her face.

"Tamar, we have gone over this before. I think that right now is the time. I think that the master will be confronting the authorities in Jerusalem and they will see, like we have, that the true Messiah is here at last. Jesus and the twelve, and a few others, left for Jerusalem two days ago and should arrive there tomorrow. I can make it there in two days and can be there when Jesus is proclaimed the true heir to the throne of David. Tamar I would not miss this for all the treasures of Solomon."

Crossing the room and taking both her hands in his, he said, "Please Tamar, why don't you come with me. It will be something we will remember all our days."

The girl slowly shook her head as she said, "Oh husband, I wish I were as sure of all this as you are. I know that I saw all that he did for you, and for others too. The things that he teaches about love and the Kingdom of the Holy One are things that could bring peace and joy to our world I know. But I have heard how the leaders of the synagogues and the Levites speak of him. I am afraid that much trouble could be waiting for him in the Holy City."

"Tamar dear, he could call a thousand angels to his side if needed, but when reasonable men hear his message there will be no need for that. We Hebrews have been waiting for this time since the time of the great kings and our leaders cannot fail to see that the day of The Lord is now here. I think that if you were feeling better you would have a better outlook on all this."

Tamar paced back and forth wringing her hands and then with hands on hips she said, "I think that how I feel has nothing to do with what you want to do. You would go to Jerusalem if I was dying."

"Now Tamar, you are getting all upset. You know I only want what is best for you. I just think that this is going to be a once in a lifetime experience for all of us. This year the Passover in Jerusalem will be the greatest ever. I just feel it in my heart that the Master will use those holy days to reveal to all the world that he is the anointed one of God."

Taking his wife by the hand, Perez led her over to the cot in the corner of the room and had her sit next to him. For a minute they sat quietly, neither one wanting to continue a discussion that might lead to heated words. Then Tamar said,

"Perez, I know exactly how you feel about Jesus and what you think might happen soon. I too have hopes it will work out,, that way but I confess I have had many doubts about how the priests will receive him. I have heard how some of the Pharisees speak of him and I think that they wish to do him real harm."

Perez was a little surprised at what he wife said as he had not thought that she had paid any attention to what the local leaders thought about such matters.

"Dear wife, if you think it would not be good for me to go to Jerusalem right now, what do you propose that we do. I feel that I must do something and not just let this whole thing just pass us by."

Tamar again got to her feet and began to pace as she talked. "What do think of this? It is about two weeks until Passover and if you are correct about when the master will be received by the priests, and the people, then you will not have to be in a hurry to leave here. That should give you time to help Uncle with the load of oil from the coast. Then if I have stopped being sick every morning, perhaps I could go with you. You know Jesus should get to Jerusalem about a week before Passover and it might be we can get some news about how he is received. If it doesn't go as expected, then we won't have to go at all."

Perez stood up and said, "I really want to go right now but I can wait a few days if it will be better for you and I suppose Uncle will be in a better humor if I make this next trip with him. He says that he makes his best profit on that olive oil that comes in from Cyprus. But Tamar, I really do mean to be in Jerusalem by Passover."

As it turned out the trip to Caesarea took longer than Perez was expecting. His uncle and he had made that journey several times but as Uncle had said, "You can always expect the unexpected on these roads."

They had been delayed twice by Roman soldiers who were looking for bandits that had been preying on travelers in that area. Then when they arrived at the coast they found that the ship carrying the olive oil had been impounded by the tax authorities until tax money arrived from the owners up at Antioch.

Uncle had been through these delays before and took them with patience and his usual tranquil nature. In fact, he rather enjoyed a couple days here on the coast with time on his hands. Time to visit a tavern and talk with old acquaintances, swapping tales of adventures on the road and at sea in the shipping business.

"Come on Perez, join us for supper and a little sweet wine. No use being impatient. Your pacing around on the dock is not going to make things go a bit faster. These bureaucrats are never in a hurry."

"Yes Uncle, I can see that they are in no hurry, but I am in a hurry to get out of this town and back on the road home. You know that I have things to do when we get back to Capernaum and then there is the trip to Jerusalem."

Uncle stroked his beard and put an arm around the shoulder of his nephew as they walked towards the tavern. "I have been thinking about this trip you plan to make to Jerusalem. I think that I can figure a way we can make a little money out of that trip. Surely we can find some goods that need to be in Jerusalem for Passover. When we get home I will go see old Jermi and see if…"

"Wait a minute Uncle. I will not have business on my mind when I get to the Holy City. Greater things than profit will be happening in Jerusalem. I want to be there when the master, Jesus comes into his glory and all the people will come to know who he really is. I know that you don't agree with me about this, but you should come with me and see for yourself. You did see what he did for me when I was so badly hurt."

Uncle nodded and said, "Yes Perez, I certainly did see what he did for you, and I think that no one else could have done that. He is certainly a great healer but being a healer does not make him a Messiah. I think that if he would just stick to healing folks, he could be a great man, and make a lot of money too. But he insists on preaching and teaching as well as healing. I don't know how all that talk is going to go over with the higher—ups in Jerusalem. They think that they already have all the answers, you know."

Perez looked at his uncle and said, "Uncle, it is what the teacher says that is really important. His ability to do miraculous things just proves who he is and that what he teaches is true. When my brother and his friends let me down through the roof of that house into the presence of Jesus, what he said first was, "Son, your sins are forgiven." Then when he healed my crippled legs all the people knew that his words were from a man of God. When the people in Jerusalem see his power then they too will know that the Messiah is here among us, right now. With Jesus as our savior and ruler, we will see our country come into its glory like it was in the days of King David and Solomon.

Uncle smiled and shook his head. "Son, I remember that there have been others who has risen up and made the claim that they were the Messiah that we have been waiting for but they have all been shown up for the impostors they were. Some of them paid with their lives; them and their followers too. If I were you I would not get too close to this man Jesus until you see how he is received by the authorities in Jerusalem. Being a hero in Capernaum and a Messiah in Jerusalem are two different things."

"Uncle, you are always seeing the gloomy side of everything. Can't you see that the Lord can do what He wants, and He wants what is best for His people. He brought the people of Israel out of Egypt and he can deliver us from the heal of Rome. My heart races at the thought of it. The first thing in the morning I am going down to the ship and insist the we get the casks of oil that we came after. Then we can get started for home."

"Perez, if that tax thing has been straightened out we should be ready to go by mid-day tomorrow. But it will do no good to go down there and get into an argument with the master of the ship. Just let me do the talking and we should be away from here as soon as possible."

As it turned out they were unable to leave the next day but did the next. During the night a storm roared in from the West tossing huge waves over the docks and smashing the ships, tied up there, into one another and against the dock. All day long Perez and Uncle watched from the tavern window, expecting to see their cargo wind up in the sea. The little boat carrying the olive oil was pushed up onto the shore but did not break up.

"Uncle, I think that the fates are with us. When this thing lets up we should be able to get the oil off of the boat and we can let the others worry about getting the boat back into the water."

17

Uncle nodded and said, "It just may be that we can tell them that we can be of help by getting part of the oil off of the ship, then it will be easier to get it back into the water. Surely the tax man could not object to that."

The next day broke sunny and bright. The wind was calm and the sea as still as a pond. All was hustle and bustle around the docks. Some of the boats were damaged and repair was needed on the pier. Perez and uncle approached the master of the oil ship and suggested that they start removing the casks of oil as soon as they could. The ship's captain agreed that it would be good to get as much cargo off as they could, saying, "You men go to it. While you are at it I will get with that tax man and explain that if we do not get the boat unloaded and back into the sea he won't have anything to tax. I think he will go along with us on this."

Mid-afternoon found the two men and a string of eight donkeys headed East out of Caesarea toward the hill country South of Mt. Carmel. Each animal carried two twenty-gallon casks of oil and Perez and Uncle were on foot. They could have loaded six of the donkeys and had two to ride but Uncle pointed out that freight paid the bills and waking was cheap.

Nightfall found them in the foothills where the going was slow, the men were weary from the labor of loading the casks and from several hours of walking and leading the sometimes-stubborn animals. Uncle knew of a spring where they could camp for the night and where there would likely be other travelers. And so, they pushed on to reach that spot knowing there was safety in numbers when out on the road in a country where bandits were known to be.

Walking at the head of the string of pack animals, Perez strained to see in the pitch dark. "Uncle, I thought you said we would be at the spring by now. Without any moon to help us we are going to be fortunate if we get there before one of us or one of the beasts breaks a leg on this rough trail."

From out of sight, back with the slowest of the donkeys, Uncle called out, "Keep your chin up son. We will be there any time now. There! Off to the right a bit. I think I see a light. It must be a fire. Someone is there ahead of us and a good thing too. I hope that it will someone that we know. It may be some of the boys from over by the lake with a load of barley."

It was in fact some men that they knew. Another group who hauled freight over these roads. They had some lumber going to the lumber poor region North of the lake. And too, there was a small detachment of Roman soldiers who were assigned to patrol the roads in this area.

When the two freight hauling groups met there was much back slapping and jolly greetings. Joking and laughing the men helped Perez and uncle unload the casks from the donkeys and turn them out graze on the sparse grass on the hillsides.

"Hey Perez," one of the men called out, "Your uncle tells me that you didn't think you were going to find this place. As many times as you have made this trip, how could you have missed it?"

"I have always come through here in the daylight. It sure looks different in the dark. But I believe that Uncle could find a gnat in the dark over these roads. He has been making this trip since before I can remember. Tell me Asher, what about those soldiers? They look like a rough bunch to me."

Asher was the leader of a group hauling barley towards Caesarea. He came over and sat next to Perez and said, "All of these soldiers look rough. I think they have to be that way to be a Roman soldier. I have never had any love for the Romans but I will admit that they make it safer in this hill country. They put up with very little lawlessness on the roads. Of course, sometimes you will meet up with some who make you pay a bribe for safe passage and they have forced me to haul their gear and pay nothing. But this bunch here is led by a fellow named Cornelius and they tell me that he is a straight arrow. One of his men told me that they expect Cornelius to make a centurion one of these days. I wish that they were all like him."

Sunup found all the men hard at work re-packing all the animals and preparing a quick meal before setting out on the road again. Perez noticed that there was a horse tied near the Roman camp fire and he had not seen it the night before. All the soldiers were on foot, he thought.

"It seems a courier has stopped over here during the night," Uncle remarked. "Those fellows can cover a lot more ground than we can with these donkeys. I think they are used to deliver messages to the scattered Roman garrisons."

Perez was intrigued by the thought that perhaps the courier had come from Judea; maybe he had been in Jerusalem. "Do you think he would know anything about Jesus arriving in the Holy City?" he said.

Uncle looked amused at the thought. "I doubt that the Romans would take notice or even care about a traveling teacher arriving in the city. Only if it caused a disturbance would he draw their attention. But of course, if you must satisfy your curiosity just ask the man. There he is over there, talking to Cornelius."

Perez walked over to the two men but was hesitant to interrupt what looked like a serious conversation. But Cornelius noticed him standing there and in a kindly way asked, "Is there something I can do for you?"

"Yes sir. I was just wondering if there was any news from Jerusalem?"

"What kind of news?"

"Well, a friend of mine went up there this week and I wonder if the people have taken notice of him. He is a man of great character and abilities and loved by a lot of the common folk. His name is Jesus."

The courier looked at Perez and asked, "Is the man from Galilee, maybe from Nazareth?"

Perez's face lit up and excitedly he said, "I knew it. The people know who he is and the Romans too. Tell me, what has happened?"

The courier seemed rather disinterested in the subject as he told Perez, "All I know is that when I was leaving Jerusalem, this man and a few men with him were coming into the city. A lot of people were making a big thing of it and were giving him a big welcome. Some were throwing their robes on the ground for his donkey to walk on. I don't know what that was all about, but I do know one thing. The man is liable to get into big trouble is those people keep shouting out like they did, "Here is the king of Israel." The commander of the troops there in Jerusalem will not take kindly to someone making a claim to be the king. I wouldn't have known his name, but I heard one of the temple priests ask about him and they seem to be unhappy with the man. I got the impression that they knew something about him before he got to town."

"Uncle, Uncle," Perez called out. "We have got to get going. Things are happening in Jerusalem and I still plan to be there."

Uncle smiled at the excitement of his nephew. "We are going, and you will get to Jerusalem. But you know with the loads on the beasts it will take longer to get home than it did coming over. Cornelius suggested to me that we should take a longer route home, going through several villages along the way. He says that the bandits are still attacking travelers on the road through the hills. I am inclined to take his advice."

Uncle was as good as his word, keeping as close as he could to the villages along the way. Perez was finding it hard to be patient and kept prodding the animals into a faster pace than they were accustomed to. By noon they arrived in a sizable town where there was a well in the center of town which gave them a chance to water the burrows and give them a ration of barley.

"You take care of the beasts and they will take care of you," said Uncle. "We should not push them too hard or they might give out before we get home. And I am not the young man that I used to be either. I have walked this road many times, I always took it at a reasonable pace."

As Perez poured out a jug of water into the trough next to the well he said, "Uncle, I have an idea. I'll wager that we could sell at least two of these casks of oil here in this town. That would free up one of the donkeys and we could take turns riding it. That would give us both a little rest. What do you say?"

Uncle smiled and said, "The major flaw I see in that plan is that the oil does not belong to us. As you well know we are getting paid just to haul it; it's not ours to sell. I sure that Lasara has this oil sold and would be very unhappy with us if we came up short. Even if we gave him the money he would not be able to fill his contracts and we would get the blame."

Perez replied with a sigh, "It was an idea I had. Maybe I will have a better one next time."

Night fall found them approaching Tiberias which lies on the shore of the lake. Both men and beasts were weary, and Uncle said that he knew of a small inn where they could spend the night. Perez would have pushed on toward home if he had had his way but after some discussion he saw the wisdom of waiting until morning. The animals drank their fill from the lake and some continued to stand in the shallows, just cooling off.

The two men found the inn and there they purchased a meal of mutton and brown bread which they ate with gusto. They mingled with the fishermen and travelers who were stopping there for the night and shared stories of experiences and mishaps on the road. When Perez told that he meant to go to Capernaum the next day then be in Jerusalem in two more days; he was treated with laughter from the group around his table.

One large man across the table slapped a big rough hand on the table and fairly shouted, "If you can make it from Capernaum to Jerusalem, on foot, in two days, I'll be the most surprised man in Galilee. On a good horse maybe, but who has a good horse besides the Romans?"

Another man chimed in, "If you are thinking of being there by Passover you should have started before now."

Perez looked disconsolate. "I should have gone on when I first said I would. Letting Tamar talk me out of it and making the trip to Caesarea just messed thing up."

The men around the table seemed to be amused at Perez's discomfort. They admonished him to pay no attention to women, they always want a man to stay home. Another advised that if he was going to haul freight for a living he would be better off without a wife, since he would be gone so much.

Perez was not amused by their laughter and he soon got up and walked outside and stood catching the cool breeze off of the lake.

Uncle soon came out and found a place to sit on a large rock near the shore. "Pay no attention to that bunch of know nothings. What they don't know about how to get along in life would fill a scroll a league long. But I will have to say that they are right about one thing; you will never get to the Holy City by Passover. Let's go on to bed and get a good night 's sleep and with an early start in the morning we should be home by early afternoon."

It seems that things never work out as smoothly as they are planed. Perez and Uncle we up before the sun the next morning but we greeted by a strong East wind blowing a sand storm that made it difficult to see more that a little ways ahead. They found the donkeys huddled in a bunch with their tails to the wind and very reluctant to move at all.

Perez stood with the hood of his robe pulled up over his mouth and nose and surveyed the situation. "Uncle, you do not have to say a word; I know that we can't move out in this mess. I just wonder how long this is going to last."

"There is no telling son. I have seen these sand storms pass on by in a few minutes and other times they have lasted for days. We will just have to wait it out. You remember the one that caught us last year. It was gone in about a half a day."

The two went back into the in inn and spent the morning playing war i, a board game popular with many of the men of the town. Many of the fishermen played the game regularly when the weather was bad and considered themselves experts. So it came as a shock to find that they were beaten handily by the young Perez. They did not know that Perez had spent almost four years as a cripple with a lot of time on his hands, just lying on his cot and spending a lot of time with games to pass the time. By dark the wind had died somewhat, and the sand was not as thick in the air and the two of them were sure that by morning they could be on their way again.

The usually placid Uncle was now beginning to be impatient and was more than a little anxious to be on their way. "I am afraid that if we have to spend too many days on the road we will not make a dinar from this trip. These innkeepers want to get ever last coin from a traveler when they know he is stranded with them. At home I could have eaten for a week on what they charged us for a meal last night. The whole lot of them are as crooked as a Roman tax collector."

Perez could hardly suppress a smile. "Uncle, perhaps a little less wine would help keep down expenses. That stuff they bring in from Lebanon may be good wine, but it adds up on the bill."

By evening the wind had subsided and while everything was covered in dust and sand the air was clear.

Perez and Uncle both were now restless and anxious to get on the road towards home. At Perez's urging they set off towards Capernaum knowing that they only had a couple of hours of daylight left. "The closer we get to home the better I know the road, he said. I believe I could do these last few miles with my hood pulled up over my head. When we settle up with old Lasara I should get enough from my share to help me get to Jerusalem. I should have already been there. I am afraid that I have missed the great day when the priests at the temple would declare the Jesus is the Messiah that we have been waiting for since the days of the prophets. But I am going anyway. We who have seen who the teacher is should be there when the whole world sees. Uncle, don't you think you ought to go with me?"

"Perez, I have told you that I am not as sure about this business as you are. You know I have agreed that he is a good man and a skilled healer, but I think that the religious leaders in the Holy City are not going to say that there is someone out here in the small towns who is closer to God than they are. All men tend to defend their own territory and religion and worship and teaching have always been their territory. They will not give up that position easily."

As Perez moved off at the head of the string of donkeys, he muttered, "Uncle, you have got to have faith, you have got to have faith."

The two kept moving as the darkness settled over them but they were both determined to keep moving and they were now on familiar ground. As the sun rose Capernaum came into view and the weary travelers were looking forward to finding their own beds for a while.

"Mother, look! It's Perez and uncle. I can tell him as far as I can see."

Tamar and her mother stood in front of the house looking down into the valley where they could see the two men and the donkey train making their way up the hill. It would be a few minutes before they got to the house, so the older woman went in to fix the travelers something to eat. But Tamar started off down the road to meet them. She could hardly wait to greet her husband she also had an anxious look as she hurried down the hill. His being away on these trips were not unusual but the young wife was always glad to see him home again. This time would be different. She knew that Perez was eager to be off to Jerusalem as soon as he could and the news from the Holy City had not been good.

Perez saw his wife coming toward them and called back to Uncle, "Here comes Tamar. Doesn't she look great. Who could guess that she is going to be a mother?"

Uncle laughed as he replied, "Son, she just found out about the baby. You have a lot to learn about these things. Give her a little more time and everyone can tell."

"Perez, it is so good to see you back safe. And you too Uncle. How did it go? Did you have any trouble? I think it took longer than you thought didn't it? Did you get caught in that sand storm that came through here?" As she plied them with questions Tamar put her arms around her mate and continued, "Lasara came by yesterday and asked if I knew when we could expect you. I think he is worried about that shipment of olive oil. I told him there was no telling when you would get here but I didn't think it would be much longer. He said that if you did not get here soon someone else would take his oil customers. I told him he need not worry."

Tamar chattered on as the three of them went on up toward the town; Perez holding Tamar's hand and the lead line of front donkey. Uncle, as usual, brought up the rear, and he called out, "We need to get this oil unloaded and then you two can talk and visit to your heart's content."

"Tamar, why didn't you wake me? I have almost slept the day away."

"Dear husband, you needed to sleep the day away, after spending the night on the road. I will venture that Uncle will not get out of bed before tomorrow. Look here, he sent over your share of the profit from the trip to Caesarea. He said it would have been more if you could have gotten home without all those delays."

Perez got to his feet and stretched as he said, "The money will come in handy for our trip to Jerusalem. I hope that you will go with me. You know what I told you about what the Roman messenger said about the welcome Jesus got in Jerusalem. I think that great things are already happening up there. Could you be ready to start by morning?"

Tamar shook her head and with serious demeanor said, "While you were sleeping two men came by who were returning from the Holy City. One of them was Justin, the little man who lives just the other side of the well. He said they left Jerusalem on the last day of Passover and that there had been some trouble in the city just before they left."

Perez asked, "What sort of trouble? Did they say?"

"He was not for sure, but he thought some men from Galilee had been arrested. He did not know who it was but was told that the priests were involved so it must have had something to do with the temple. Maybe some of the Zealots were causing trouble again. I think that this might not be a good time to be in Jerusalem. If there is much of a disturbance in the city the Roman soldiers will take matters into their hands and you know how they treat anyone that they suspect."

After much discussion, Perez reluctantly agreed to delay the Jerusalem trip for a few days, or until they had some reliable news from there. "Uncle said that he knew of some men who should be coming home shortly and they could tell what was going on there. These fellows go up to the City every year at this time. With all the travelers coming to Jerusalem at Passover it is a good opportunity to sell food and even clothes and they do a good business in sandals. They have been at it for years and know everybody there. They will have the straight story on what is going on up there."

It was noon of the next day when three of Uncle's friends arrived back in town. They went straight to Uncle's house and were fairly bursting with news.

Justin leaned in the window of Uncle' s house and called out, "You know Simon don't you, the fisherman. "

"Certainly, I do," replied Uncle. "I have known him for years, except he does not do much fishing these days. Most of the time he is traveling around with that healer, Jesus. Why do you ask?"

Uncle asked the men in and they told what they had seen and heard in Jerusalem. "You are right. Simon was in Jerusalem with Jesus and the priests had Jesus arrested and hauled before Pilate. It all took place in the dead of the night and they had him convicted and executed before noon of the next day."

"What in the world did the man do to cause him to be executed? I know that some of the Pharisees did not like some of his teachings but that is not a capital offense. You know my nephew, Perez. He thinks that Jesus is God's man in the world. In fact, he thinks that Jesus will be recognized as the Messiah, and now you say that he is dead."

Another of the men spoke up. "It may be that Messiah business that got him in trouble with the religious leaders but they said that Pilate accused Jesus of trying to make himself a king. I heard Jesus teach when he was here in our town and I don ' t think that he made any claims about being a king. I just do not understand it at all."

Uncle looked out the door and said, "Look, here comes Perez. He is going to take this news very hard. He put a lot of faith in the man, Jesus. He fully expected Jesus to be welcomed at the temple as a Messiah or at least a great teacher. I hate to have to tell him the news."

Perez hurried into the house and went straight to Justin. "Greetings friend. Tell me, what is the news from Jerusalem? Did you get to see Jesus and his companions?"

"No Perez, we did not see Jesus, but heard some bad news about him."

"Bad news? What bad news? What has happened?"

Justin then told all that they had heard, just as he had related it to Uncle. Perez was stunned at what he had heard and blurted out, "You must be mistaken. This terrible thing could not have happened to Jesus."

"I am afraid it has son. We even heard that Simon and the others who were with Jesus, are in hiding, for fear of their life."

Perez slumped down onto a bench near the door. "How did they kill him? Surely not by stoning."

One of the men said, "We heard that he was crucified. Someone told us that his mother was there and witnessed the whole thing."

For a while the men stood quietly the only sound was the groaning from Perez. The young man looked up and said, "I have talked to the rabbi about the coming of the Messiah and he told me that the prophets said that the true Messiah would be despised and rejected by many. I knew that many people did not accept Jesus' teaching, especially the Pharisees, and I thought that confirmed what the prophets had said. Now they have killed him. Could a true Messiah be killed? Would the Lord of the Hebrews allow such a thing?"

Uncle and his friends stood silently. They had no answers for Perez.

The following days were hard ones for Perez. He kept busy helping Uncle bring a load of grain up from Tiberias, but his heart was not in his work. Tamara did her best to cheer him up by talking about the expected child and her plans to enlarge their sleeping room in the coming months. But all of their talks usually got around to Perez's disappointment in the establishment's failure to see Jesus for who he really was.

"Tamar, it could be that I was wrong about Jesus being the expected Messiah. God would never let the Messiah suffer the fate that he met. But I still know that he was sent by the Almighty with a message for all the people. How else could he have the power and the grace and the love that he had for everybody. I am still going to try to live the way that he taught us. Somehow I think that the man will never be forgotten."

Tamar took her husband by the hand and said, "You could do a lot worse than living by the teachings of Jesus. I remember how he talked about forgiveness and loving the unlovely. Some of those teachings will be hard to follow but if we all did, wouldn't it make for a happier world?"

"Perez! Oh Perez!" someone shouted from outside the house where the couple were talking.

Perez got to his feet as he said, "That sounds like cousin Jerimy. I have not seen him in weeks."

Perez and Tarnar went to the door and sure enough, it was Jerimy. He was tying his donkey to a post by the door and giving a big smile of greeting to them. "Peace to you both," he called out. "Could a weary traveler find a little rest and refreshment here?"

"You are most welcome friend. Come on in and Tamar will bring something to eat."

Tamar took Jerimy by the hand and led him into the house as she said, "Cousin Jerimy, it is so good to see you again. Tell me, how are the wife and children? They are well I hope."

"When I left they were all in good shape. The boys are   like tares in a wheat field. The oldest is almost as big as his mother now."

Perez smiled as he said, "Tamar has something to tell you about our family, don't you dear."

Jerimy looked at Tarnar and said, "I'll bet I can guess. Would I be right if I said that your family is about to increase?"

The three sat and talked of family and friends for sane time and then Tamar asked Jerimy if he would spend the night with them.

"It's nice of you to ask Tamar but I had better get going soon. I can be home by dark if I get on way soon."

Perez asked, "Where have you been Jerimy?"

"I had to go down to see about my mother in Jericho and while I was in Judea I went on to Jerusalem for Passover. And Perez, have you heard about what happened to the teacher, Jesus?"

"Yes, we heard. And think it is the worst thing have ever heard of. The best man I ever knew and they killed him like a common criminal. I told Tamar that I think his teaching will live on but it is a great tragedy. When Simon gets back to Capernaum I want to talk to and find out how it all happened. Did you see Simon or any of the other followers of the teacher while you were there?"

"Perez, do you mean that you have not heard the latest about Jesus?"

"What do you mean, the latest?"

Jerimy stood up and began to pace as he talked, "I heard from some men that I did not know that Jesus had been turned over to the Romans and that they had executed him, for treason they thought. Then a few days later as I was leaving the city I happened upon James. You remember him, the fisherman and one of the group who were with Jesus. James told me that they had seen Jesus alive, and this was after they had seen him buried and some of the women had seen him taken down from the cross and were sure he was dead. James said that a man named Cleopas had seen Jesus and had eaten with him, and this was three or four days after he was executed. Do you remember Mary, from Magdala? He

33

says that Mary says she talked with Jesus while standing outside of the tomb and this was three days after he was supposed to be dead. I don't know what to make of it all?

Perez jumped to his feet and declared, "If what you say is all true then I know what I think about it. I think that we who thought Jesus is the Messiah were right all along. Where do you think he is now?"

Jerimy shook his head. "That I do not know. I know that his disciples, the ones who went with him to Jerusalem are still there, at least I think they are. James did say that he thought they would be coming back to Galilee soon. But to tell the truth, he seemed to be unsure what they would be doing and about exactly where Jesus was at that time."

Perez turned to Tamar, "Wife, you and I must to go Jerusalem. I am more convinced than ever that great things are going to happen there. If the Teacher is alive I want to be there and see him and hear him again."

Tamar replied, "I am beginning to think you are right. If you wait a few days, then we can be there for Pentecost. We can take our offering to the Temple and then hopefully we can see Jesus. It should be a glorious time."

"Tamar, you are right. We will be there for Pentecost and it will be a memorable one."

The Boy Jesus

Luke 2: 41-51

"Greetings Sara, I see you are home. I was beginning to worry. We thought that you would be home two days ago. Or by yesterday at least. Did things go well at Passover this year?"

Sara took a seat on a bench on the shady side of the house and let the bundle she had been carrying slide down between her feet. "Yes, Mariam, it was moving and inspiring time. I will admit that I am tired. I told my husband that if I go next year he will have to find a donkey for me to ride or at least to carry our clothing and food. I just don't hold up to these long trips like I used to. Why didn't you go up Azo the Temple this year?"

Mariam sat down next to her friend and said, "You know that Melchi's mother has been sick lately so she could not make the trip, so I told him just to go on with his friends and I would stay with the old lady. Actually, I enjoyed those days with the husband and the boys gone. I just had to fix for the two of us. I spun a little wool and repaired my good robe and just rested a lot. Tell me, why were you gone so long this time?"

"Oh Mariam, we had a scare. You know that we were traveling with a large group, mostly relatives. My cousin,

Joseph, and his wife, Mary, and, their oldest boy, Jesus, were in our company.

When we left Jerusalem, starting for home, all the children were staying together, playing and having a good time like they always do. A lot of them are cousins, you know. It was a fine day, clear and not very hot, so we made good time. Got all the way to the olive grove near that nice spring where we planned to spend the night. Well, Mary got to looking for Jesus when it was time for the evening meal. She just knew that he was with some of the relatives he was not to be found. Joseph got some of the men to help look but no one could remember ever seeing Jesus after we left the city. By that time, it was getting dark some said it was too late to start back to the city to look but Joseph insisted on going back right then so a few of us went with them. I'll tell you, traveling on that Jerusalem road in the dark is hard business. We were fortunate that it was a clear night with enough moon to give us some light."

Mariam, who was listening in wide eyed amazement, asked, "Well tell me, did they ever find the boy?"

"Yes, we did, but it took a couple of days and then we lost a day getting home so that is why we are about three days late getting home."

"Sara, where was he all that time?"

"Can you believe it? He was at the temple all that time. Joseph and the other men had looked there two or three times but there is such a crowd there at Passover they just didn't see him. Then Mary overheard some men talking about a boy who had been in discussion with some Levites and scribes and had greatly impressed them. Mary asked the men to describe the boy they had seen Mary knew that it was Jesus. She had heard Jesus talk about spiritual things many times as he had matured, and she knew of no other young man it could of been."

"Did they just go inside the Temple and find him there talking to the elders."

"They did just that. Mary said that Jesus was sitting with about a dozen men and was talking just like he was one of them. But by then she was so upset with the boy that grabbed him up by the back of his robe and led him out of the place with his feet hardly touching the ground."

Mariam smiled and said, "I'll wager that Joseph took a stick to the boy."

Sara looked serious and replied, "No he didn't. He and Mary talked with him and explained how he had greatly worried them, but Jesus replied that he felt that he should be doing that sort of thing. He made a boyish mistake but at heart I think that he is a fine boy."

"You know Sara, that Mary has always thought that her oldest was somehow something special. She has never told me all about it but I know that some unusual things happened about the time he was born. You remember that don't you?"

"Yes, I remember. They do think that their son is destined to be someone special I suppose all parents think that way. I do know that he is well thought of by most that know the family. I think that he will turn out well."

Return Home

"Momma! Momma! Look there. That looks like Uncle Joseph coming up the road. Didn't you say that we didn't know what had happened to him?"

The woman turned and looked in the direction that her son was pointing. Coming toward them was a bearded man leading a burro on which sat a young woman. Running along in front of him was a small boy who looked to be about three years old.

"Mercy me! That does look like Joseph and Mary too."

The woman threw down the cleaning rag she had been carrying and ran to meet the group coming up the road towards her. The woman on the burro slid down to the ground and the two women fell into one another's arms in a tearful embrace.

"Mary, brother; what happened to you? What happened to you? Where have you been? We all thought something bad must have happened and maybe you might be dead."

Joseph embraced his sister and said, "Jecol, a lot has happened to us and much of it was bad. But some wondrous things have happened too."

Jecol took Mary by the arm as they walked towards the house, and she said, "Joseph, you left here over three years ago to go to Bethlehem to be enrolled and we have not heard a word since then. Mary was in a family way and, oh, this must be your little boy. Isn't he sweet. Come here to your Aunt Jecol. What 's your name deary?"

The youngster looked up at his aunt with the confidence of a boy who had been many places and seen many things. "My name is Jesus and mother has told me about you and uncle Silas. When we were in Egypt my father told me...

"When you were in Egypt? What do you mean Egypt?"

Joseph spoke up. "Yes Jecol, we have been to Egypt and we will have to tell you all about it.

Jecol turned to Mary and said, "Are these two telling me the truth? Is that why you have been gone all this time?"

"Yes dear. They are telling the truth, and it is a very complicated and amazing story. A story that shows the wickedness of man and the grace of the Almighty."

The four of them reached the house and as Joseph tied the burro and took a bundle from the animal's back, Jecol chatted on and plied them with questions. "We heard that old Herod had ordered some children in Judea to be slaughtered and I was afraid that you might be involved in that. I am glad that that wicked man is dead."

Joseph looked serious as he said, "We are glad that he is dead too, and that slaughter is the reason that we fled to Egypt. He had all the little boys in Bethlehem killed so we left there in a hurry."

Jecol led them into the house and lit a candle to chase some of the gloom from the small room. Then with hands on hips she demanded, "Why would he want to kill little boys. And why would you go to Egypt instead of just coming home. We did not have that trouble here."

With a little smile Mary replied, "Jecol, there is much to tell you and much of that I think you will not understand. In fact, some of what we have to tell you may not even believe."

"Of course, I will believe whatever you say. Now tell. . ."

Joseph interrupted, "Jecol, who is doing the carpentry work here in Nazareth now? Is it Silas?"

"Oh no. Silas worked at it for a little while, but he didn't like it. He only tried because some folks insisted that he build them some furniture. He did help build one barn. He soon let Manasseh take over that job. You remember him, lives over on the other side of the hill. He is not really able to work much anymore and is older than Mount Sinai. I think you can start right back into the business. Silas, as you know, is never happy unless he is working with his sheep and goats."

With a worried look Mary asked her sister-in-law, "Who is living in our old house? Do you think we will have to find another place?"

"I think that you will be all right there. My sister moved in there about a year ago when we decided that something must have happened to you. But she understands that it is Joseph s place and I suppose she will move back in with me. Now you must tell me before I die of curiosity, how could you afford to go to Egypt and stay there all that time?"

"Come right here and let's sit down," Mary said. "I have things to tell you that will amaze and touch you too."

"What sort of things would astonish me more than just you showing up after all this time?"

Mary seemed to be looking at something far away as she quietly said, "Let me tell you about angels, Eastern Magi and heavenly choruses. Jecol have you ever seen real gold or myrrh. Oh my dear, I have so much to tell."

The Wise Man

"Good morning Father. Are you well today?"

"Yes daughter, I am getting about very well this day. My knee is doing much better, and I have been seeing about the camels. The animals are all in fine health and are ready to go whenever I am ready."

"Why are you out here looking at the animals? Surely you are not still thinking of making the trip back to the West, back to the land of those Hebrews. And we have heard that the Romans have many warriors there and they may not be friendly to travelers from our country."

"Yes daughter, that is my plan. I hope to..."

"But father, think of you age, your health. That is too much for a man alone. I know that you say that you know the way, but it has been thirty years since you and the other went there."

The old man sat down on a low wall in the shade of an olive free and said, "I realize that it has been thirty years and all my friends from that journey are now gone but we all agreed that someday we should return to see what has come to pass in these many years. We knew that the Hebrews look to only one god and that god seemed to speak to us years ago. I told you of our dreams and..."

"Yes father, and the star, many times. But does this god still speak to you? Do you have a word from him now?"

Her father smiled and replied, "I must admit to seeing no new stars, nor have heavenly agents spoken to me, but there is a pull to know; did the child become a prophet in his God's family. We know that he wears no jeweled crown or lead an army, or we would have word of it. But the Hebrews are looking for something deeper than that. This need to know the fate of the child may come from what Caspar called The Spirit."

Taking a seat next to her father, the woman took his hand and said, "I understand this desire father but remember your age and how you have those spells. I fear that if you go you will never return. The first time you were gone many months and you had help from the others. I also recall your telling about being threatened by that king in Jerusalem."

"Yes dear, I am aware that my years are slipping away; and that gives urgency to my task. If I don't return what better way is there to send my soul to eternity than to lose it while seeking knowledge of an eternal God?"

"Father, if your mind is set on this I do not know what more to say."

"You can wish me godspeed my child and say a prayer to the one who sends me on this journey in search of enlightenment. You know my old companions would come with me if their spirit was still in the body. I believe I can still feel their presence as I prepare to go."

"But father, after thirty years, the child who was to be blessed by God could now be anywhere. How can you find him?"

Looking at his daughter, he replied, "I will trust that the spirit that urges me to go will show the way. In over thirty years the child, now a man, will have had some influence in that country. I expect to find him well known. Now, bid me farewell; I will be off with the dawn."

A Mother Healed

Mark 5: 25-34

"Mother, where have you been? We have been worried sick about you. You know you shouldn't be out in the hot sun this time of day. Now why don't you come on in and lie down for a while. The doctor said that you would never get better if you don't take care of yourself."

"Oh Maria, I have been into the village and a most wonderful thing has happened."

"You have been into the village? Mother, I cannot believe that you walked all that way by yourself. And on a day when there was such a crowd there. Jerez told me that that teacher from Nazareth was there and there were so many people in the streets he could hardly get through to pick up a cask of olive oil. What were you doing down there?"

The two women moved around to the shady side of the house and sat on the wooden bench there. The older woman took her daughter's hand and with shining eyes she proclaimed, "Maria, I am well. I am well. After all these years the blood has stopped, I feel like a new person. I walked all the way home and did not stop to rest even once."

Maria looked at her mother in astonishment. "Mother, what do you mean, you are well? How could you get well in just a day? Yesterday you were just barely able to drag around the house. Now you say you can walk all over the country. Did something happen to you in the village?"

"Did something happen to me in the village? Let me tell you about it."

The older woman stood up and began to pace back and forth and talk with a passion her daughter had never seen in her mother. "Maria, I have been suffering for at least ten or twelve years now. The bleeding never stopped and every doctor I have ever seen never did me no good. In fact, I have gotten worse over the years. You know that. Everyone says that I have gotten as pale as a new lamb and I know that I have been weak as a kitten the past several years."

"Mother, I know all that. But why do you say that suddenly you are so much better? I will admit that you do have a good color today and I can't remember when you have had so much spring in your step."

The older woman sat back down next to her daughter and said with much emotion, "For a lifetime I have been attending the synagogue and hearing the elders read from the law and the prophets. How many times have I heard the words of Isaiah,

Those who look to the Lord will find new strength
They will run and not be weary
I will strengthen you, I will help you

I concluded that it was time that I took the word of the Lord seriously. While I was meditating on these words of the prophet I began to hear of the teacher from Nazareth, Jesus is his name. I heard from good sources that he was able to heal all manner of diseases. They told that he was a compassionate man who had a special love for poor folks like us. So I decided that I must go see him when he was in our town, and that is what I did. Now look at me, good as new."

As she spoke the woman sprang to her feet and whirled around with her hands high over her head.

"For goodness sake mother, be careful. You are going to fall and hurt yourself. Tell me, did you just walk up to this man that you had never met and ask him to treat you? That would be a rather familiar thing to do."

"No daughter, I did not ask him to do anything for me. As I walked toward the village this morning I prayed that the Holy One would guide me, tell me how to approach the teacher. When I saw the great crowd that was following him I knew that I would not have a chance to talk with him but the feeling came over me that if I could just touch him it would be enough; and it was enough."

"Mother, don't tell me that you just walked up to the man and touched him and it made you well; and what did people say to you about your walking up and touching a strange man in public?"

"No dearest, I did not really touch him. There was such a crush of people around him that I could hardly get to him but as he passed the corner where I was standing I was able to just barely push in between two old men and I reached out and with just one finger I touched the hem of his robe. And then he just stopped, and he said, "Who touched me?" For just a minute I thought he might have been offended but that was not the case. He had the sweetest look on his face and he said, "Daughter, your faith has made you whole. Go in peace, "and he said that I will never have this trouble again."

Maria shook her head as she said, "I just do not know what to think about this whole thing. Mother, do you really think that you are well of your hemorrhaging. And do you think that the teacher, Jesus, was the one who cured you? And who is this Jesus anyway?"

Putting an arm around her daughter, the mother replied, "Yes, I am really free of that disease and yes it was the power that flowed from Jesus that made me well. Who is Jesus? I know that he must be something more than just a good teacher. I think that he is someone special with God. The word Messiah comes to mind but I am not sure about that. I just believe, I know, that he is God's man in the world."

Apostles' Discussion

Luke 9: 46-47

Winter was definitely on the way. A cold wind blew across the ridge top and the men pulled their robes up tighter in a losing effort to ward off the chill. The man in front walked alone and appeared to be lost in his own thoughts, while several yards to his rear was a group of about a dozen or so men who were in animated conversation.

"I will certainly be glad when we get into Capernaum. I have a heavier cloak there. This thing that I have on has about chilled me to the bone." The speaker was a tall thin man who was making an effort to cover his head and face as he leaned into the biting wind.

"Now Matthew, you are just soft from sitting too many years behind a tax man's table. I say that a few seasons in a fishing boat would toughen you up. Andrew and I have been out -in worse than this and handling a wet net to boot."

Matthew turned towards the speaker and replied, "Yes, I know Peter. You are stronger and smarter than the rest of us. I know that because you are quick to tell us. But I also know that what is needed in our mission with the teacher is a dedication and a skill in spreading the message that some of us have more than others."

Peter turned to their companions and said, "Did you hear that? Matthew would have us believe that he is better at speaking than I am. And you know that no one can question my dedication to the master. Furthermore, I think that he recognizes that and will soon put me in a place of authority in the work."

There was some muttering and head shaking in the group and then one of the youngest of them spoke up. "I have been with Jesus as long as anyone here and James and I have more experience working with people than any of the rest of you. You will remember that we had several men in our employ in the fishing business. But more importantly, we have spent more time close to the master than any of you. Peter, you may be the biggest and the loudest of us all, but when Jesus decides to pick leaders for the kingdom he has been telling us about, then he will pick those of us who know him best."

The group had now reached a place where the road was sloping gently down and the ones who had been walking near the rear caught up and one asked, "What have you been talking about? Are you still trying to figure out who the teacher is going to make his right-hand man?"

"I'll tell you what I think he ought to do. (It was Simon who was reputed to be one of the zealots, who was speaking) The master should appeal to the people who want to see our beloved land free of the accursed Romans. I could put him in touch with a number of men who would join with us in a minute if only Jesus would be more specific on how he would bring in the Kingdom Of God that he speaks of. Am I not right Bartholomew?"

Bartholomew frowned as he stroked his beard. "I am not sure about that Simon. I hear him talk a lot about love and forgiveness and even loving our enemies. That does not sound like something that your Zealots could go along with.

And what about humility and being a servant to others? We know what he has said about those things."

Peter turned around to Bartholomew who was walking behind him, "It is well enough to be a servant when you have to but being a servant and being a leader are two different things. A good leader can recruit men to be servants. I know that Jesus is a humble man who does not push himself to the front, and I say that is the reason why he needs a forceful man to work closely with him. With all humility I think that I am that man."

Andrew, who was walking a little way ahead of Peter began to laugh. "With all humility, you say. Brother, what do you know about humility? I think that Bartholomew is right. Our master talks a lot about loving others, even or enemies. It will take someone who thinks like that to be the one who sits at his right hand. In fact, I wonder if he will pick one of us to be. more important than the rest. Jesus does not put much importance on personal gain or glory. You remember that many times he has asked us not to tell who had done a healing or other miraculous work. What do you think Judas?"

"I think that this wind is about to cut me in two. We have a little money in the common purse and I am going to suggest that we buy some heavier robes. Things like that need to be thought about and I am the one to do it. The teacher should ask me to be his personal steward. What do you think?"

Bartholomew frowned as he said, "I can't help but remember what he said about not taking an extra cloak as we go about our mission. Material things or comfort, for that matter, are of not much interest to Jesus. I say that if he did choose someone to be his special assistant it would be someone who does not concern himself with coin or extra

51

clothes. It would have to be a man who has a passion for spreading the word about the Kingdom of God and doing good for the common man. Who that man might be, I do not know."

Andrew looked around and waved a hand toward the group. "I think that all of here have a passion for the master's work, but some of us are better leaders than others. Some of us have shown that we can heal but we have also failed at times. Having an ambition to be at the right hand of the master calls for a special talent and a special concern for the poor. Something more than most of us have, I'll wager."

"Speak for yourself Andrew. I have the passion. I have the ability to speak. I have the ability to lead and inspire. And I have the courage to lead when things are not going well."

"Yes, Peter, and the humility also."

Sabbath Busyness

John 2: 13-16

They were four rather old gentlemen and they had been friends for as long as they could remember. They were sitting on a low stone wall that was in the shadow of an ancient fig tree. The top of the wall was worn smooth by much use and these men were a common sight there as they played wari, a board game popular with older man.

"Perez, that was not a good move. Now Salmon will go out on you. But of course, he always does."

With general laughter in the group, Perez said, "You are right there. I have not won a game since I last played a game with my wife, and now she won't play with me."

Salmon was the oldest of the group and by general consent the wisest. He turned to the two who were watching the game and said, "The Rabbi at the synagogue down the hill says that we should not be playing games on the Sabbath, but I have never seen anything in the law to support that. What do you think of that Ahaz?"

Ahaz was a tall, very thin man who looked as he had never been pleased with anything in his life.

"I think that the law keeps changing over the years. When I was just a boy there would be a game of wari going on under every tree in town and, I do not remember that anyone complained about that. I think that every rabbi has his own idea what is lawful on the Sabbath. Of course, some things are written in the law but most are what we might call the oral law and every priest and rabbi has their own idea about that."

Eliud sat down to take his place at the game board and turning to Ahaz he said, "You are right about things changing and sometimes for the better and sometimes not. Do you remember about thirty or thirty-five years ago when that fellow from up in Galilee chased the dealers in sacrificial animals out of the temple. He had his notion of what was not right to do in the temple and there were several people who agreed with him but not much changed."

Salmon nodded and said, "I was one of those who agreed with him I did not say too much about it. You will remember what it got him. There are times when it does not pay to say too much."

"You are right about that but about the trading of animals, I think that there has been some changing of attitude about that. More of that sort of things goes on out on the roads now and less right inside of the temple," Perez said. "I do not know if what that fellow did thirty years ago had anything to do with that change or not. What do you think?"

Ahaz spoke up, "Maybe it got the priests at the temple thinking about what is appropriate and what is not. But when it affects how much money certain people can make then change can come slowly. I could be that some people had to die before any real change could be made and Perez you are right when you said that there has been some change in the trading of animals but the changing has been minor. The folks doing business out on the road are the small fry. The ones with the connections are still in the temple and will be as long as it is profitable."

A Torn Family

"Jothan, we are going to have to do better than we have this morning if we are going to get this barley in before the rain comes. And you can't get anything done by staying in the shade all day."

Jothan the hired man dragged himself to his feet and said, "Sir, why am I the only one out here today? Where are Silas and Azor. If we beat the rain, we are going to have more help than just the two of us."

Eliud was a tall straight man with a perpetual grim expression on his face. He looked at his field hand, Jothan, and then gazed around the field before saying, "You tell me Jothan. Where is everybody? If those two have run off just when things are busy, then they just can stay gone. I will not have them back. You go over to the house and see if they are there. If they are, you tell them it will go better for them if they get right back out here."

Jothan started back toward the house while his master Eli ud began to sharpen the scythes that would be used to cut the ripened grain. As he worked he thought to himself, "It is not right that all the responsibility for the farm should fall on my shoulders. It's not as if I can't handle it. No one works

55

harder than I or gets more from the servants and field hands. I know that father can no longer do hard work but that no account brother of mine should be here and helping. He never was known as a hard worker he would be better than nothing and he does have the knack of knowing where to find help when it is needed on short notice."

His musings were cut short by a shout from Jot han as he came hurrying down the hill towards the threshing floor where Eliud sat.

"Well, where are they?" Eliud asked.

Jothan had to take a minute to catch his breath and then said, Sir, before I got within sight of the house I could hear someone playing a harp and cymbals. Just like they were having some sort of celebration and out near the cattle shed I found the house servants and Silas and Azor. They were dressing one of the calves that your father had us put up and start feeding so they would fatten up. And sir, there is good news."

"Well, spit it out man. What news is so good as to cause father to kill a fatted calf?"

"Your brother that's been gone so long. He is home. Your father says for you to hurry home and help welcome him back. I think that he has invited some of the neighbors, as well as your uncle and his family."

Eliud's face was dark with anger as he turned away from Jothan. He stood and looked in the direction of the house, debating with himself over what he should do.

Wheeling about he fairly shouted at his hired man, "Yes, I will come to the house; but not to celebrate the home coming of a prodigal. I will be there to let him know what I think about a man who would squander all that a too generous father let him have. Whores and strong drink have taken away half of what it took this family years to gather and a leather whip would be too good for him."

Eliud started toward the house with a purposeful stride and a set face. When he reached to top of the hill in view of the house he could see his father standing at the door and looking down the road in his direction; as if waiting for his eldest son. He was.

As soon as Eliud reached the front gate his father came out to meet him. The older man moved slowly and with obvious pain in his feet or legs.

"Eliud my son. Have you heard the news?"

"Yes, father I have heard, but I am not as happy about it as you seem to be. One of the house servants just told me that you ran down the road to meet him, and now look at you. You can barely walk."

"Oh, Eliud, I had to go…"

"You had to go meet the one who took his share of the estate early so he could squander it in every evil way he could think of. You know all the stories that have come back to us from that heathen country. And I dare say that they are all true."

"But son, he is still flesh of my flesh. How could I not welcome him home?"

"I'll tell you how you could welcome him home. Put a hoe in his hand and send him out to chop the tares out of the field beyond the spring. Send him out to find the donkey that has been missing for three days now. I dare say that in a few years he could work out what he owes you."

The father slowly shook his head and in a low voice said, "My son, your brother owes me nothing. I freely gave what he asked for and now he asks for my forgiveness and I freely give that also."

"Father, you are very generous when it comes to your footloose and immoral son. But I have failed to see that generosity when you are dealing with me. Now tell me, where is the boy?"

"He is in the house with his friends and the family. Have you not heard the music?"

"Yes father, I have heard the music. It makes me wonder when we have had music with some of my friends or when we have had a fine calf to eat. I do not remember even having a goat to use to make merry with my friends."

"My son, my heart is always glad that you always faithful and true with me. It should take no celebration for you to know that. Everything that is on this place is yours to have and enjoy, but I have to rejoice when a son that is lost is now found. Wont you come on in and share in our joy?"

As Eliud turned he said back over his shoulder, "Tell the prodigal that I will be glad to see him at sunup, in the barley field. And tell him to bring his scythe."

A Father's Thoughts

Mathew 4:21-22

"Greetings Zebedee, I was told that you might could use some help today."

"Peace to you Matea. Come on down. You were told rightly. It is just me and the nephew today."

The tall Matea climbed down the bank to the boat where his neighbor sat repairing a sail. It was a still foggy morning and the sun was just beginning to come up over the hill across the cove from where the boat was tied.

Sitting down on the side of the boat Matea said, "It looks like it will be a good day Zebedee. The sun will burn this fog away shortly, and they tell me that the catch has been good lately."

"I appreciate your coming to help today," replied Zebedee. "My help has all gone up to Jerusalem for the feast of Passover. I suppose that I should have gone too but you must fish when the fish are here and as you said, they have been fairly jumping into the net these past few days. If we do well today, Matea, I should be able to pay you a liberal wage."

"That sounds good to me. Working in the vineyards has not been very lucrative this year. I felt like I should stay home myself this year. You know, it costs to make that trip and it is doubly hard when you miss some work. I suppose that your sons are in Jerusalem. I know that the teacher they have been following goes up for all the feasts."

"Yes, I am sure that they are in Jerusalem now, but you can never be sure. Since James and John have taken up with that Jesus you never know where they might be. In the past two or three years they have been in about every town in Galilee and Samaria. Even making regular trips to Judea."

Matea began to fold the nets into the bow of the boat and he turned toward Zebedee and asked, "What about this fellow Jesus. Some say that he is a prophet from God. Others say he speaks against the beliefs of our fathers. And I have heard stories of marvelous healings that he has done. What do you think?"

The fisherman did not answer right off. He pushed the boat off of the gravel bank and climbed into the stern as soon as the boat was afloat. Pulling on the line that raised the square sail he tied it off and then settled back with one arm over the tiller.

"Matea, I will say right off that I think that Jesus is a good man. He is an honest man who does what he thinks he should be doing. Sometimes he speaks a little too frankly and it is going to get him in trouble one of these days. I suppose that you could say that he is a rabbi, at least a teacher. My sons think enough of him that they, as you well know, just walked away from our business here on the lake. I was disappointed that they left just when we were doing so well but I said very little against it. They were determined to go and anything I said would just start a family argument."

Zebedee pulled the tiller to bring the boat about to run with the wind as his helper began to prepare the nets to be let down. Matea had been on fishing boats on this lake many times and there was no need for instructions. Both men knew their jobs well.

As he let the net slip over the side Matea said, "I can see why two young men who were idealistic and wanted to serve the Holy One might come under the spell of a teacher and miracle worker but you know that the people in the village are saying that your wife too has become a follower of Jesus."

Zebedee had a rather stern look when he replied, "It is none of the business of the village busybodies what my wife thinks or does. Salome is a woman with a mind of her own and some resources of her own. She has seen fit to help her sons as they have been traveling and helping teach what they see as the word of the Lord. She and some other women are in Jerusalem for the Passover and I would think that she will see her sons there."

Matea gave a tug on the line to the net to see if it felt heavier. Feeling nothing, he sat back and then said, "If I know Salome, she will see that Jesus gives her sons good positions within that group that are working and traveling with him. I remember that when James wanted to work for old Jethro that time, she insisted that he be allowed to run the boat and that did not set too well with the old man."

"Yes, I remember that. She always did have high ambitions for the boys, but I think that I have seen some changes in her and the boys also. Jesus talks a lot about humility and putting others first. I know that is a hard lesson for some to learn but they put a lot of store on what the man says."

"Do you think that your sons will be coming back home soon? Don't you think that they will want to settle down with a wife and family?"

"I have thought a lot about that. I hope they will come back and take over this fishing business. We have always made a living at it and they know that they can do well. But…well, it seems that they have made a serious commitment to their mission. I really except them to be gone for a good while yet. But one day when Jesus moves on to other things I guess they will have to come back. A man can't spend a lifetime just traveling around and teaching. Quick Matea, check that net. Let's get back to paying attention to important things."

The Priest's Story

Luke 10:29-37

From Elymas, priest serving in the first month, at the Temple of the Most High.

To the most esteemed Gedaliah, friend of many years.

Knowing that you will be coming to Jerusalem for the Feast of Booths I wanted to let you know what events have taken place to cause me much embarrassment.

Perhaps you have heard of a certain Jesus, an itinerant teacher and trouble maker from a small town in Galilee. It is bad enough that he makes claims to be someone special with the Heavenly Father (he claims for himself the title, Son of Man) but he blatantly criticizes those of us who are teachers and serving in the temple.

He seems to have a special animosity towards the Pharisees and I will admit that they deserve some of it. You know how they feel superior to we Sadducees. A stiff-necked bunch they are.

But the man has gone too far. One day he was telling a group of Levites how they should practice generosity and charity and he used me, Elymas, as a bad example of a charitable person. Oh, he did not use my name but everyone there knew who he was talking about. In fact, some had already been talking behind my back about an incident down on the road to Jericho. But of course, they did not know all the facts in the case, and none had the nerve to confront me personally about it.

When I was on the way to Jerusalem to begin my term of service there, I came upon a man lying in a ditch beside the road. He was in bad shape. In fact, he looked like he had been in a brawl. Most of his clothes were gone and he was bleeding badly. Now this Jesus person told about a priest who had found an injured person on that road and had refused to render aid. No doubt he was talking about me and I resent the fact that I did not get to tell my side of the story.

As you know I only serve in the temple a few weeks of the year and I go to a lot of trouble to arrive there in good order. I always acquire a new robe and, on the days, preceding my journey to Jerusalem I am careful to do nothing that would make me unclean. Furthermore, it is important that I arrive there at the appointed time. When I came upon this fellow in the ditch, I of course felt a certain pity for him but on reflection I determined that there was nothing that I could do for him. I certainly could not arrive at the temple with blood on my robe and that would have happened if I had tried to pick the man up and carried him anywhere. And it certainly would have taken some time to do any good for him because we were not close to a dwelling where I could have secured help. Furthermore, there was no way to be certain, without handling the man, that he was not a Samaritan or even a Gentile.

I had no other choice but to go on my way because the important thing was my service at the temple. I am sure you will agree that this was my only choice. Later I learned that a Levite had made the same decision and that convinced me that I had done the right thing.

I am sure that would have been the end of the affair if Jesus had not brought the matter up and compared me to a Samaritan, of all people, and told how the Samaritan had helped the wounded man and that had made him a better and more charitable person than I. I am just as charitable as the next man but sometimes the work of the Holy One in the temple has to come before helping a peasant in the countryside.

I think that I saw that Samaritan rather soon after I left home. I soon got ahead of him as he was leading a rather scraggly ass and appeared to be in no hurry. And I did not want to be seen traveling along with his kind. They say, or at least Jesus did, that the Samaritan took the injured fellow to that inn near Sycar and left him there. What difference does it make to a man like that if he gets blood all over himself? He said that the Samaritan even paid for the man's care at the inn. What kind of care could a person get at a country inn? He would be about as well off still in the ditch. I Say that the injured man must have been a Samaritan himself or he would not have gotten that much help.

Feeling that I had been unjustly maligned I went to see Gamaliel. He is, you know, a member of the Sanhedrin and I think that this Jesus ought to be brought before them and have to answer for his libelous talk. Gamaliel was of no help at all. He asked if Jesus had called me by name and of course he had not. Then he asked me if I had in fact passed by an injured person on the road. I then set about to explain the circumstances as I have set them out to you. But the man would not listen to reason. He is just a teacher with his head in the clouds who does not see the world as it really is. He would have us scurrying about seeing what unfortunate person we could help and then the work of the Most High would never get done.

I apologize my friend for making you read of my troubles but when you come to Jerusalem and hear talk of me I wanted you to know the truth of the events.

Stephen and the Mob

Acts 7:54-60

"BLASPHEMY! BLASPHEMY!" The shout rang out from the mob as the victim was dragged from the meeting place of the Sanhedrin.

The man Stephen had had the audacity to say to the governing body of the Jewish nation that they had been responsible for the death of the Righteous One, the promised Messiah.

Now there was a rope around his neck and a rod prodding him in the back as he was dragged from the city to a hill on the outskirts of town.

Stephen was stripped of his clothes before being shoved into a shallow depression with the howling mob all around. Some of the younger men picked up small stones and hurled them quickly, all trying to be the one to cast the first stone. Most of them to little effect but one caught the victim in the face and a small trickle of blood ran from the corner of his mouth.

Then a large man of course appearance stepped forward and removed his outer robe and threw it at the feet of a younger man named Saul. "Since you are just going to stand and watch, you can guard this for me."

Striding towards Stephen the large man yelled to the crowd, "We didn't come here to just entertain the people with our rock throwing skills. We came here to execute this man who blasphemes the word of the Most High." Taking a stone half the size of his head the man threw it, sticking his victim below the chin and sending him to his knees.

An animal like roar went up from the mob and only the ones closest to Stephen heard him say, "Lord Jesus, receive my spirit."

With that the stones rained down from the crowd. One small boy was pushed forward so that he could throw one and they all laughed when the boy missed his target.

Blood was pouring from every part of the martyr' s body when he collapsed to the stony ground.

"He is done for," someone shouted. "He has gotten what he deserved," another said.

"No, wait, he lives and is speaking," said a man who had come close to take a look at their victim.

Stephen could hardly speak with blood coming from mouth and nose and ribs broken so badly that they protruded through the skin. The man Saul stepped close enough to hear and years later he reported that Stephen said, "Lord, lay not this sin to their charge."

Also hearing this was the big man who had struck the first damaging blow. He turned to the mob and cried out, "The man still blasphemes. He must die now!"

As he said that he selected a stone that took both hands to carry. Standing over the martyr, the stone was crashed down upon his head. Then it was obvious to the mob that their aims were accomplished. They had killed the one who dared criticize their long-held beliefs. The following days they would tell one another that a man who defended one who claimed to be the Messiah deserved to die.

On a Sabbath soon after that in a nearby synagogue, there was study of the 32nd Psalm. The leader read "Blessed is the man whose sin the Lord does not count against him." Then turning to one next to him the leader said, "Brother Saul, what comment do you have on this Scripture?"

Saul hesitated for a moment before saying, "The Psalmist also said, "I will confess my transgressions to the Lord—and you forgave the guilt of my sin."

"I am still considering my transgressions."

And he sat down

.

A Shared Lunch

John 6: 1-13

"Jannia, where have you been? You said you were going down to play with your cousin, Heli, and you have been gone all day. I have been worried sick."

"Oh mother, it has been a fine day, a magical day. You should have been with us. You just will not believe what happened today."

"Son, I hate for you to be gone all this time and have to depend on my sister to fix you something to eat. You know that they do not have a lot to spare."

"She did fix us a lunch but nothing too fancy. When we told her that we were going to go along with the crowd to hear the teacher from Capernaum she gave each one of us some bread and a couple of pieces of fish. And I have got to tell you what happened to that lunch. You just will not believe it."

The woman laughed and said to the boy, "That's twice you have said that I would not believe what happened today. Now tell me what it is that I will not believe."

"Mother, you have heard of the teacher that has been going through our area and healing people and tell them about God, haven't you?"

"Yes."

"This morning, he stopped at the house right next to Heli's and he healed a crippled girl that lived there. And you never saw so many people. They were all excited and talking and yelling, some were even crying. When he left he headed up toward that high hill across the valley from there. And you never saw such a crowd that went after him. Aunt Sari said that it would be all right if we went along too. She said that we could tell her what went on, and if anybody else got healed. That's when she fixed us the bread and fish to take with us."

"So, you and Heli followed the crowd up on that high hill. What is so unbelievable about that? Did you see him do some sort of miracle or something of the sort?"

"Mother, we sure did. We saw him do the most amazing thing you ever heard of. He took my lunch and he scattered it around to the crowd and there was enough for all of them to have plenty to eat. And there was a lot left over too. There must have been thousands of people there and they got all they wanted to eat and it all came from my lunch. What do you think of that?"

"Jannia, what I think is that you are making up a wild story. Maybe three or four people got a bite or two from your little basket of bread and fish. What put it in your head to tell such a tale as that?"

"Now come on in the house and calm down. You can tell me what really happened up there and you don't have to make a big story out of it."

Jannia and his mother went into the house out of the late afternoon sun and as Jannia got a drink of water from the jar sitting under the table the woman said, "Now what in the world happened that kept you boys out all day. I have seen several people come by here today and some of them were talking about hearing the teacher, but none said anything about being fed while they were with him."

"Mother I'm telling you the truth when I say that something wonderful happened up there today. I think that the teacher, his name is Jesus, went up on the hill because there is a lot of grass there and it is a good place to sit down. He talked all morning about how the poor people are loved by God and how sad people are going to be made happy and a lot of other things that I can't remember right now. But what he said was not the magical thing, it was what he did with the food."

"Now Jannia, you are not going to tell me again that he fed a thousand people with your lunch, are you?"

"Yes Mother, I would take an oath that…"

"Son, why would he decide to take your little bread and fish if he was going to feed a lot of people? If he did I suppose that he got the lunches from a lot of the folks there. Maybe everybody there had a bit of food with them and that is why they all had something to eat. At least that would make more since than saying he fed all the people from one little basket."

The boy put down the cup that he had been drinking from and said, "I'll tell you just how it happened. One of the men who was with Jesus is called Andrew. He is a really nice man. He told me that he is a fisherman and he showed me some knots that they use when making up their nets. I think that now he spends a lot of time going around with the teacher, Jesus, helping him do stuff I guess. Anyway, when it got to be about noon we heard Jesus tell Andrew and some other men to get some food for all the people there. One of the men said that there was no food there and if there was it would take more money than they had to buy it. That is when

Andrew went over to the teacher and told him about the bread and fish that I had in my basket. Andrew knew about my lunch because I had offered to give him a barley loaf that morning. Jesus, the teacher, asked me for my food and I gave it to him. Then the really magical thing happened."

Jannia's mother laid her hand on the boy's arm and asked, "What happened that was so magical?"

"I'll tell you. He took the bread and held it in his hands up over his head and then prayed a prayer and began to break it into pieces. He just kept on breaking the bread up and the men started passing the pieces out to all the people and they kept at it until everybody had some bread. Then he did the same thing with the two fish. I mean everybody there got some bread and- fish from the stuff that he got from my lunch. I saw it with my own eyes. And Heli saw it too."

The woman gave a deep sigh and replied, "Son I know that you would not just make up a story like that, but there must be some explanation of how that happened other than it being a miracle or some kind of magic."

"Mother, look out there, the boy said. Is that Melki out there with a big basket?"

An elderly neighbor was approaching their door carrying a large basket that was almost more than he could handle.

The mother went to the door and asked, "Melki, what in the world do you have there? Do you need some help with that basket?"

A big smile came on the neighbor's face. "Look here. See what I have got?"

The woman looked in the basket as her friend sat it down. "What in the world? This looks like a basket full of cooked fish."

"Sure is, and I thought that you might like some of it." There is more here than the wife and I can eat before it goes bad. And here comes Haggi and he has a whole basket full of bread. I know he will want to give you some of that too."

Jannia's mother looked at her son and then at the basket of fish and them at Haggi lugging his load of bread. "Son, you said that something happened that I would not believe. Well. I did not believe at first but now it is obvious that something strange has happened. Melki, tell me. Have you and Haggi been up on the hill where the man Jesus was teaching today?"

"We sure were. We were there with him all day. And wait till I tell you what took place."

The woman laughed and replied, "You will not have to tell me. I think I already know."

Scene at the Well

John 11: 1-44

Mariam arrived at the well right at dusk, just as the sun dropped behind the Judean hills. Several of her friends were there and she was glad to see them. She had been away from Bethany for several weeks attending to a sick brother who lived in Joppa, over at the edge of the great sea.

"Greetings Mariam," one of them called as soon as she drew near.

"Peace to you Shamar," replied Mariam. "How are you all? I am so pleased to see you. It feels like I have been gone for a year."

Mariam set her water jug on the stone paving near the well to await her turn to draw from the only well in the small town. But she was in no hurry. Coming to the well in the late afternoon was a social occasion in the town, as in most towns in the Judean countryside. It is where the latest gossip is exchanged, where you found out about new babies and whose marriage might soon be arranged.

"Let me have a sup of that while it is still cold," she said as her friend Hermine pulled her large pot over the edge of the well. "All the water I had at the house has been there for at least two days and is as warm as broth."

Mariam looked around and said, "I haven't seen Martha today. I thought sure she would be down here."

Some of the women there smiled or giggled but Hermine got a real serious look on her face.

"Mariam, I don't know what to think about Martha and that flighty sister of hers. You remember, I 'm sure, what happened about a week before you left. She had all those strange men from somewhere up in Galilee staying around her house all day. She even fed the whole bunch. And that Mary tells that the leader of that group is a teacher, some even call him Rabbi."

"Oh yes," Mariam said. "Mary said even more than that about that fellow, Jesus. Claims that he has healed sick folk and talked like he thought he was the Messiah or something. Yes, that happened just as I was leaving. They haven't been back in town, have they?

One of the other women spoke up. "Yes, they have been back and I am surprised that you haven't heard about it. I mean, that's all that has been talked about around here ever since."

"Well, don't keep me in suspense. What happened that would cause so much talk. Martha is not going to marry one of them is she. Or maybe Mary. I remember that a couple of them were rather young, about her age."

"Oh no," replied Shamar. "It is wilder than that. You recall that Lazuras had been kind of sick for some time. Well, he took a sudden turn for the worse. In fact, he got really bad. So, Martha sent for this Jesus, who was over on the Jordon River somewhere. They had the notion that Lazuras could be cured by this man. They said they sent for him right away, but it was four days before Jesus and his group got here. They did not seem to be in any hurry about it. By the time Jesus arrived Lazuras was already gone. Or they thought he was."

One of the older women, Monas, spoke up, "I went to the house when I heard that Lazuras was dead and I am here to tell you that he was gone, I mean he was definitely dead. I know some folks say that he was in a coma or something, but I know what I saw."

"Now Monas, how do you explain the fact that he is walking around the town this very day as if nothing had ever happened to him? What do you say to that?" Shamar's voice was getting a little louder as she queried her friend, Monas.

"Wait a minute," spoke up Mariam. "Monas said that she saw him dead and she has seen a lot of dead people. Now you others are telling me that he is not dead. It sounds to me like something strange has happened or maybe one of you is getting to be a little strange. Tell me what this is all about."

Shamar sat down on the wall of the well and began her story. "About three weeks ago was when it all happened. Like we told you, Martha sent for this Jesus and when he got here they already had Lazuras in the tomb, the one where the rest of the family are interned. You seer they were all sure that he was really dead."

"I'll tell you the body already had an odor and 1…"

"Hush Monas, I'm telling this. We want Mariam to get the story straight. They thought he was dead so when Jesus came Martha fussed at him for being so late getting there. Told him that if he had been there sooner, he could have done something but it was too late now. Then this Jesus told Martha and Mary both that their brother was not dead, that he could walk right out of that caver and sure enough he was right. Jesus stood up there on the hill across from the tomb and called to Lazuras and he came right out of there like he had never been sick."

Mariam had a puzzled look. "But if even if he was not dead wasn't he so sick and unconscious that he could never walk out of there alone?"

Hermine spoke up. "I was there the day that Lazuras came out of the tomb and he looked well to me once they got the grave clothes off of him. He told his sisters that he felt good except that he was hungry. It had been several days since he had had a bite to eat. Some say that Lazuras came back from the dead and that Jesus was the one that did it. I say that if Jesus only caused him to get well it was some kind of miracle."

Monas spoke up again. "If you don' t believe Lazuras was dead just ask the family that lives next to Martha. They came over and prepared the body for burial and you can believe me when. I tell you that his body was beginning to stink. My husband helped carry him up to the tomb. Nearly everybody in town will tell you that something happened here that they had never seen before. I think that the Holy One worked through the Galilean and did a miraculous thing."

"If the man was really dead and the man Jesus called him back to life, then what does that tell us about Jesus? Who is this Jesus?" asked Mariam.

"Perhaps he is who Martha says he is. That day she called him the Messiah, the Son of God. He would have to be something like that to do the works he does. You should hear some of the things that Mary says that he has done. A lot of people here in our town think that he is someone special from the Holy One. But some of the men have told the priests in Jerusalem what has happened and what people are saying about Jesus. They are not going to like it if he makes claims of being a Messiah." Hermine spoke this with mounting conviction.

Mariam let her water pot down into the well and as she drew it out and placed it upon her head she said, "Friends, I want to hear more about this and I think I am going up to Martha's house in the morning. I want to hear it from her myself. I know that Mary may be a little imaginative, but Martha is levelheaded and I would put a lot of confidence in what she tells me."

Shamar smiled at her friend and said, "Believing that a dead man is now alive and well will take a lot of believing. Nothing like that has happened since Ezekiel was in the valley with the dry bones."

Mariam called back as she walked away, "Maybe we have another of the Holy One's prophets with us again."

Zacchaeus

Luke 19:1-10

"Philip, have you seen the others? I went to see about getting some food for the evening meal and now I can't find any but you two."

"Here Andrew, have a seat. It's cooler here in the shade. And you will not have to worry about getting very much food for tonight. The master and the rest of the group have made arrangements to eat at the home of a man here in Jericho."

Andrew put down his bundle and stretched out in the grass under the shade of the olive trees. "It does feel good to take the weight off my feet. That is the roughest road I ever saw coming into this town. Every rock in the road seems to be standing on edge with its sharp edge up. How come you two are not with the master if he is going to eat in one of the homes here?"

Philip looked over at the other man who was sitting in the grass leaning back against the trunk of a large tree. "Judas and I were just talking about going to join them. We know that it will not do our reputation any good to be seen there but if the teacher is going I guess that we can too."

Judas spoke up. "That Zacchaeus is a crook and everyone in town knows it. I do not know why the master invited himself to that man's house for a meal. And, oh,

Andrew if you had any money left from buying the food I will take it."

Andrew leaned over and handed Judas a couple of coins and then asked, "Do you mean Zacchaeus the publican that I have so much about? That fellow has a reputation all over this area."

"The very same," Judas answered.

Philip spoke up, "I cannot help but remember what the master said one time when he was criticized for being friendly with people who were seen as sinners. He said that he came into the world to treat the sick, not the well, or words to that effect."

Judas shook a finger at his two friends and said, "I will tell you what I think. I think that this Zacchaeus is trying to polish up his own image by having a man like Jesus come to his house for a meal."

Philip looked thoughtful as he said, "You know it was Jesus who first mentioned going to Zacchaeus' house. Andrew, we were walking through town and there was the usual big crowd of people along the way. Suddenly Peter took me by the arm and pointed up into a sycamore tree. There siting on a limb was a little old man who turned out to be Zacchaeus the publican. When the master saw him Jesus got a big grin on his face and he yelled out, "Come down from there Zacchaeus, I must go over to your house today."

Andrew said, "I would say that some in the crowd did not look with favor on that."

Judas got to his feet as he said, "It set most of the crowd grumbling about Jesus going to visit a notorious sinner. And I will have to say that I did a little grumbling about it myself. But on further reflection I can see that some good can come of this meeting. They say that he is a wealthy

81

man and it may be that he could be persuaded to help with the finances of our work. It takes a certain amount of cash to feed and house a dozen or so men on the road, even with the hospitality that we sometimes receive."

"Now Judas," Andrew replied. "You surely remember that early in the work he sent us out to carry the message and told us not to take a purse but to depend upon hospitality. I do not think that he would accept money from the man."

In an exasperated tone Judas said, "You are probably right. That is one of the things that bother me about the man. He is not practical about things like that. How are you going to bring in the Kingdom if there is little money to get things done? What little we have he would have us give it to the poor and at the same time he says that we will always have the poor with us. That way coins pass through our hands like sand."

With a smile Andrew replied, "Perhaps he can persuade this fellow Zacchaeus to give some to the poor. From what I hear he can afford it."

"Ha, that will be the day. You know as well as I that it is the poor who listen to the teachings of the Master. The rich people think that they do not need to hear him talk about love and forgiveness. And you have heard him talk about the virtues of the meek. Meek is not what this Zacchaeus is."

Philip looked at Judas and said, "Judas, my friend. I hope that you are not getting as cynical as you sound. We have left home and followed Jesus because we believe that his message of love and repentance can change people, even Zacchaeus. And if Zacchaeus can be changed, then the world can be changed."

Andrew said, "I think some of us have stayed with Jesus because we have been changed ourselves. I know that I never give a thought to the price of fish anymore, and I used to worry about that every day. Making a living is not what most of us think of these days."

The three men all got to their feet and began to gather the bundles.

"Let's get into town. I am sure that the master is expecting us to be at Zacchaeus' home tonight," Philip said. "And who can tell, we may learn something."

Writing

It was busy as usual around the outer court of the temple. The hot Judean sun beat down on worshipers and pilgrims as they arrived bearing their offerings of money or animals to be sacrificed on the alter, as they and their ancestors had done for a millennium.

In this multitude were two women in animated conversation. "Mona, I was here myself yesterday when the rabbi from Galilee was teaching, right over there, in that shady place. Most of the folks who heard him seemed to be impressed with him, except some of the priests, of course."

The other woman frowned and shook her head and replied, "Cleo, I don't know how much confidence we can have in an itinerant country teacher. I heard that the authorities brought in a sinful woman who had—well, I don't like to talk of such things. They said that the priest asked the Galilean what should be done with her and the teacher persuaded them to just let her go. Did you see that?"

"Yes, I was standing right over there and could see them but could not hear all that was said. In fact, the man did not appear to have said much at all when the priests quizzed him about how the poor girl should be punished. I did see him kneel down and with his finger, or maybe a small stick, write something in the dust."

"Cleo, what in the world could he have written that could have caused the priests to change their mind about that person? Did you see it?

"No, I didn't see what he wrote; but let's go over there and see if it is still there. Though I doubt that we could still see it with so many people trampling around here."

The women made their way over to the stone bench where the Galilean had sat as he taught the crowd.

"Right here is the place and you can still see a little bit of what looks like writing there in the sand but doesn't look like anything we can read."

"No, it's been walked over too much, but look there; you can make out a little something there. What does that look like to you?"

Cleo bent over to get a better look and then said, "It just may be the word, "give". But what would that mean? Give what?"

"I don't know what the teacher would want them to give her, but, wait; what if the whole word was "forgive"?"

"Mona, I think you are right. From what I have heard about the Galilean teacher that would fit right in with his teaching. My brother, Asa, said that he heard the man teach that we should forgive like we would want to be forgiven. Now I am really curious to know what else he wrote."

After Supper

Luke 10:38-42

"So, you finally show up in the kitchen. After they are all gone you come back here like you want to help. I'll tell you Mary, I am still vexed with you."

The younger sister looked at Martha and replied, "And I am unhappy with you too, embarrassing me like that."

Martha set down the kettle she had been using to clean some serving bowls. "What do you mean? Me embarrassing you? All I did was try to get a little help when I was trying to show some hospitality to our guests. I am sure you know that was the most people we have ever had in this house and there you sat as if you were a guest yourself."

Mary picked up one of the serving bowls and as she dried it she said, "You came right into the front room and in front of the rabbi and all his friends you asked him to make me help you with the entertaining. I think it was rude of you to put Jesus on the spot like that."

Martha was about to make a reply when into the room came a man who looked like the two women except for being several years older.

Martha turned to him and said, "Lazuras, what are you doing in here? Don't you think that you should be resting? You know that this has been a long day for you, sitting out there talking and listening to the master since this morning."

The brother dropped down onto a bench that was against the wall and replied, "I had to come in and see what you two were talking about. You were beginning to sound a bit shrill."

Martha quickly said, "We were discussing the fact that I have been nearly worked to death today while you other sister couldn't seem to find time to help me."

"Now Martha," Mary spoke up, "I know how hard you worked today but the Master was teaching us some things of eternal importance. You should have joined us. You heard him say that it was important that we hear him. In fact, he said that it was needed."

"Mary, I am not disputing that what he says is something that all need to hear. I am aware that Jesus is a man sent from God and I would not want to miss a word of his teaching. But I know also that it is a woman's place in this world to serve and take care of her family and friends. I cannot be with him all of the time. There are things that have to be done and that is the sacrifice that I must make."

Lazarus spoke from his place on the bench. "It is one thing to be a hostess and another thing to be a gracious hostess."

Martha put her hands on her hips and asked, "Just what do you mean by that brother?"

"I just mean than when you are entertaining a gracious hostess makes it look effortless. She doesn't want her guests to think that they are a bother by being there."

"And just how do you make it look effortless when you have a dozen or more men to feed, and these men have just worked up their appetite by walking several miles to get here?"

As she said this the older sister went over and took a seat beside her brother. "Lazarus, I am not arguing that I did not want to hear the master teach. I very much wanted to but I think that everyone has their duty to perform and I think that I have found mine. Now tell me, what was he teaching about today?"

Before Lazarus could speak, Mary, who was leaning against the work table said, "Oh Martha, I wish you would have come in to hear him. He had a lot to say about forgiveness and loving those who are hard to love. He told a story about a Samaritan man who helped a Hebrew in trouble and said that was the way we are supposed to treat all people, even foreigners."

Lazarus joined in, "The master talked a lot about the Kingdom of God and about how we all may be a part of it, but I confess that I did not understand a lot of that. But if he is going to be the head of that Kingdom I want to be a part of it. And Mary, what was that he said about us being like little children?"

Mary came over close to Martha and said, "Martha, he said that we should be as humble and believing as little children and as eager to learn and believe. One time he even took the little neighbor boy on his lap and said we must welcome little children just like we welcome him. It was the sweetest thing I ever heard. Oh, it will take me a long time to tell you all that he said this day. Martha dear, I will make you a solemn promise. When Jesus comes back through town I will do all the kitchen work and let you sit with them and hear all the wonderful things he says."

With a small smile Martha replied, "I will hold you to that dear, but I am still not sure how it looks for a woman to be spending the day with a group of men, some of which I do not know very well. But if the master says that it is needful maybe I can risk what the neighbors might say. At least for one time."

A Changed Man

Matthew: 9:9-13

"Levi! Levi! Wait just a little, I will walk over with you."

The older man stopped and turned to wait on his friend. "Hurry Melchi. I must get along. I have guests coming to the house for dinner this evening."

Melchi fell into step with his neighbor of many years and said, "I heard that you were having several people in for a feast tonight. It is some kind of celebration or is it business with your fellow publicans?"

Levi kept up his quick pace as he replied, "There will be several of my business acquaintances there as well as family and other friends. Why don't you come too? I think you will know most of the folks. There will be one man there that you should get to know. Jesus is his name and he is from over at Nazareth, even though he spends a lot of time around Capernaum these days."

Melchi could not have looked more surprised. "Are you talking about that Jesus that claims that he can heal sick people? If you are having him over to your house I can tell you that it will not make you very popular with the Pharisees that do all the talking at the Synagogue. Not that you eare very popular with them anyway, I mean, well, you know what I mean. I don't mean to offend you but. . ."

"Yes Melchi, I know what you mean. And no offense is taken. I knew when I got into the business of collecting taxes for the Romans that I would lose some of my friends. Many of them say that I have not only betrayed our people but that I have offended the Almighty as well. Be that as it may, that part of my life is all behind me now."

"What do you mean by that? Are you going to take another region? I thought that you were doing real well here. At least you live like you are doing well."

Levi stopped and laid a hand on his friend's shoulder, "My friend, I have given up the profession all together. Something more important and closer to my heart has been calling me for some time and just yesterday I made a clean break and turned in my franchise. From this day forward I will devote myself to the leaning and teaching the message of repentance and righteous living, as taught by my new teacher, Jesus."

"Your new teacher? The man is a carpenter, they say. And he is always traveling about. If you are his pupil I doubt if you • will be around enough to enjoy owning one of the finest houses in this town. Levi, are you serious about this?"

"I have never been more serious in my life. Listening to Jesus' teaching caused me to examine the way I was living and what was important in my life. I discovered that extracting taxes from my countrymen was what took most of my effort and thought. He teaches that we are to love others as much as we love our self and I saw that cheating a neighbor was the antithesis of that. I saw that I had hardened myself against the hatred that many of the townspeople feel towards me. Melchi, I now know that I cannot go on living like that. Somehow I must begin to love so that they will love me."

"And Melchi, tonight I am going to introduce the teacher to as many as will come to my house to dine. I well know that some will criticize him for dining with me and I pointed that out to him. But do you know what he said to that? He just smiled and said, "Levi, I will be pleased to be there, you will be pleased, and the Father will be pleased. We must just do what is right and trust that good will come from it."

"Come now Melchi, we must hurry. I have a lot to do before it is time to dine. Do you think that you will be there?"

Melchi appeared to be giving it serious thought and then he said, "I may just do that. And tell me, could I get your tax franchise?"

A Plan Gone Awry

They were gathered in a small ante-room of the Temple. About a dozen of the chief priests and Caiaphas the high priest were in a good mood, laughing and talking about the comings and goings around the Temple that day.

One of the men who sitting facing the door cried out, "Look who is here. I believe that our old friend, Amon, is back."

Silhouetted against the sunlight streaming through the door was a man whose appearance was so striking that he was instantly known by the group. "Greetings and peace to you all, "he called out in a jolly voice. "May I join this esteemed gathering?"

Amon was a priest of long standing. He was short of stature and very near as broad as he was tall with a mere fringe of white hair above his ears. His bald head was bright red from the sun which made him stand out among a mostly swarthy skinned populace. A Jew originally from Greece, he had been in Jerusalem most of his life and risen in the religious establishment.

"You are welcome," cried one of the younger men.

"It is seldom we get to speak with a blue-eyed priest."

There was general laughter all around as the new comer took his seat.

93

Caiaphas stood to greet Amon and said, "It is good to see you back again my friend. You look as if a few months at the sea shore did you a lot of good. You do have more bounce in your step than you did when you left here."

Amon nodded and smiled. "Yes, I am feeling a lot better and I am glad to be back. What is the news? What has been going on here in the holy city in my absence?"

At that question the mood in the room turned somber. Caiaphas' expression was grim as he said, "Much has happened in recent days and you will be glad to know that a threat to the beliefs of our fathers has been squelched. I think that you will remember that there was a group of men from Galilee who were teaching things contrary to the Law. The leader of that bunch was called Jesus, and he was heard on more than one occasion to say that the law concerning the keeping of the Sabbath could be ignored."

Amon looked puzzled as he replied, "Why Caiaphas, I am surprised that you would let the man get away with that sort of thing."

"We most certainly did not let him get away with it. The man has now been in his tomb for three days and his followers are scattered to the winds."

One of the other priests spoke up. "This Jesus also talked of a coming Kingdom that was supposed to be of God, but of course it was he, not the Temple priests who were to be in charge of this kingdom. And you should have heard how he talked about his betters. One time he called the Pharisees white washed tombs, full of dead men's bones. He even accused some of them of breaking the law for their own profit."

Amon said, "I am surprised that the people would stand for that kind of talk."

"Oh, the common herd," Caiaphas replied, "thought that he was a miracle worker. You know how it goes. One or two claims that he cured them of some ai lment then the rumors start going around that he could cure anything."

"You say that you did away with this fellow?"

"We sure did Amon. Had him hanged on a cross, just like a common thief.

Amon considered that for a moment and then said, "How could you execute the man for breaking one of our laws; even for slander. Don't the Romans hold that prerogative for themselves?"

"You are correct Amon. But what we did was to get the Romans on our side in this matter. You remember we said that he talked a lot about a kingdom. We stressed that point to old Pilate. We pointed out that if there was to be a kingdom there would have to be a king and you know what the Romans think about a rival king."

"You say that Pilate had him crucified, just like that?"

"It was a bit more complicated than it might sound in the telling. We had to arrest him at night so that the rabble would not cause trouble if they saw it happen. And finding out where he spent his nights and identifying him in the dark took a little doing. But as luck would have it one of his own followers helped us out there."

"Yes, but we had to cross his palm with some silver before that happened. Just find your man and then find his price, that's what I say," spoke up one of the priests.

Just then a servant of the chief priest appeared at the door. "Sir a man is here to see you." Then coming closer he said in a low tone, "Sir I think it is that Judas that you paid the money to."

Caiaphas looked around at his associates and with a shrug said, "I think we have no more business with this man. He just thinks he can get more money from us." Turning to the servant he said, "Tell him that we cannot see him today, or any other day."

The servant was hardly out of sight when the group heard angry shouts and cursing from the outer hall. Then to their surprise silver coins rang out as they bounced across the floor. Tomas, the servant came scurrying into the room, shouting, "The man is mad. He threw all that silver at me, shouting that he betrayed an innocent man. Then he turned and ran out wailing like a wild animal."

"Caiaphas, what are we to do with the money? It is silver that has been used to bribe a man and I think that the law would declare that it is unclean?" All of the group nodded in agreement with that sentiment.

The high priest looked around the group and with a voice of authority said, "We have been looking for a place to bury the destitute and Gentiles. I think that thirty pieces of silver should be about enough to buy that place they call the Potter's Field. Don't you agree?"

Agreement was what the high priest expected and agreement he got. One of the younger priests went to help the servant gather up the silver and see that it was all accounted for.

This was hardly done before another priest joined them and it was obvious that his mood was not good.

Caiaphas looked to the door and saw that the newcomer was Annas, his father-in-law who had been the chief priest a few years back and still was very influential in affairs around the temple.

The whole group stood as the older man entered the room.

"Wasn't that Judas I just saw running from the court yard? He looked disturbed. Has there been more trouble?"

Several of the men answered at once, "No sir, there has been no trouble. We will see that fellow no more and for good measure we have all the money back that we paid him."

Annas looked even more grim. "Didn't you put a guard around where that Jesus was buried?"

"Yes we did," Caiaphas answered. "Just to make sure that his followers would not try to make a martyr out of him by claiming that he was not really dead. Or maybe they would have some other man go about claiming to be Jesus and that some miracle has occurred. With the guards there no one could make that claim."

With rising anger in his voice, Annas fairly shouted, "Caiaphas, the body is gone. The guards are making fantastic claims about supernatural beings that came and over-powered them and took away the body. Now there is no telling what people will be saying about this whole affair. I knew I should have handled this whole business myself."

Annoyed by what he felt was an intrusion into his authority, Caiaphas replied hotly, "What difference does it make where the body is? The man is dead, and everyone knows it, and furthermore the guards will be punished. Let's not let this thing upset us. It is over and done with. Jesus is dead, his followers have run to only heaven knows where and I for one think that we have heard the last of this whole thing."

Annas looked around at the gathered priests and said, "I just had an interesting conversation with Nicodemus, a member of the Sanhedrin, and a man with some insight into

97

what goes on among the people. He thinks that those men from Galilee have started something that will be harder to stamp out than we think."

"Ha, that is all he knows. Those men and their leader will be forgotten before another Sabbath. Mark my words!"

God's Man

Acts 9: 10-19

"Ananias, oh Ananias, are you here?" The man stood at the door of the small shop in the city of Damascus he received no answer from within.

From across the narrow street a woman called out, "He is not there. He left just a bit ago. Said he was going over to the house of Judas on Straight Street."

Most of the residence of Damascus knew Ananias. He ran a shop where he sold reed pens and ink. The pens he made from the reeds that he cut from the margins of the marsh land just South of the city. Black ink he made from a mixture of soot and a thin gum and this mixture was set out in the sun to dry into small cakes. The cakes would be moistened with water for use. Red ink was made from a mixture of red ocher and thin gum. The ocher was dug from the ravines near the town.

He also sold some papyrus that he bought from traders coming up from Egypt.

Ananias was a short stout man whose graying hair make him appear older than his actual years. His hands were usually stained with the ink that he crafted as were his clothes on most days.

The visitor turned to the neighbor across the street and asked, "Why is he going all the way over there? I didn't know that he and Judas were even acquainted."

The neighbor lady walked out into the street as she said, "Now you know I always mind my own business and try not to hear what is going on with the folks on the street. I was just making conversation you understand, and I asked him why the hurry. He told me that he had been called to go see a man who had been struck blind out on the road from Jerusalem."

The man looked surprised as he replied, "Why would they call Ananias? He is not a doctor; he is a seller of ink and other stuff they use to write with. Who is the man that went blind? You said "struck" blind. Do you mean that he went blind suddenly?"

The woman, named Dora, moved up close to the man and in almost a whisper said, "Minaver says that Ananias is a member of that group that they call The Way. This man who has gone blind was supposed to be on the way here to put down that group. Minaver said that someone told her that a bright light and a great noise hit the man and down he went, and now he can't see."

"Sounds to me like he was hit by lightning."

"How could it be lightning? It hasn't even rained around here in weeks. Look here comes Minaver now. Maybe she knows some more about all this. Not that I am interested of course."

Minaver was short, round, bubbly woman who greeted them with a laugh and a boisterous salute.

"What are you two talking about here in the middle of the road. Someone I know I'll bet."

Dora tried to put on an air of unconcern. "Oh, nothing much. Just wondering about that man that Ananias is going to see."

Minaver looked pleased to talk about it. "You have come to the right person to find out all about that. My brother was over there in that part of town when they brought that Saul into Judas' house. Saul was the name of the fellow who went blind. What's more, brother says that Saul was on the way here to arrest some of those folks who are part of that religious group called The Way. And I suppose you have heard that Ananias is part of that bunch."

"Yes we have heard that, but what puzzles me is why they would call Ananias. It must be a trick to get him over there and arrest him. I just happened to notice that no one has been in his shop this morning. Who came by to ask him to go over there anyway?"

Dora asked. "What do you think about that Ananias? I mean he was always a pillar in this town and now he is an outspoken member of that fringe group. Do you think that he has gone over the edge?"

The man spoke up. "Ananias is a good man. Still attends the synagogue. I suppose he has some different ideas about The Most High and some other ideas about the Messiah but I think he is a solid citizen."

Minaver said, "I think that bunch are all different. They go to the synagogue on the Sabbath and then have their own worship service on the first day of the week. What is that all about?"

"What I think is, you ladies ought to ask Ananias to tell you what he believes. He would be glad to tell you, even at the risk of being arrested."

Minaver looked grim as she replied, "If The Way is a good thing why are the priests at Jerusalem trying to do away with it? I say that Ananias has gone astray and that Saul, blind or not, is about to catch up with him."

Dora said, "I dare say we will know before night what happens over on Straight Street. Or it may be that no one will ever know and the blind fellow will just be taken back to Jerusalem and that will be the end of that."

The Centurion

Acts 10: 1-48

You could tell that he was a soldier, even when he was not in uniform. His bearing, his manner of speaking, while kindly was from a man who was used to being obeyed. The scars on his face, especially the one that ran from the corner of his left eye to his chin showed that he was no stranger to warfare.

Cornelius was a centurion in the group known as the Italian Cohort and commanded one hundred men that were stationed in and around Caesarea. He was pleased to be in that area of the Roman Empire after many years of service in other areas. His slight limp was the result of toes being frozen in a winter crossing of the Alps during a campaign against the Gauls. Three winters in that wet and cold land were enough to keep him from ever wanting to going back to Europe. Some of his men thought that it was too hot here on the East end of the Great Sea but then they had never crossed the Alps in the cold months.

Hot and dry was just fine with him. Old wounds ached less in that climate.

Cornelius had not been there long before he married a widow with two sons and the domestic life, after many years in barracks was a great comfort. His wife was Jewish and he was soon drawn to the teachings he heard from his new relatives. She and her whole family had a peace and a sweetness about them that was a new experience to him.

One day on the last day of the week he accompanied his wife's brother to meeting at the local synagogue and there a revelation came to him. One of the older men stood to read the lesson of the day from an old manuscript. The centurion heard things like, "Thou shall not kill and Thou shall not seek revenge or cherish anger towards your kinsmen."

Thou shall not kill! It rang in his ears. He had spent a life time in the killing business and teaching others to do the same. Not with any real hatred toward others, it was his duty to the Caesar. It was what a soldier did.

Do not seek revenge! Cornelius had learned that not to avenge an attack was to invite another. But these people, these Jews, taught that their God expected them to live this way. Not that they all did. Some were looking for an opportunity to take revenge on the armies of Rome but many tried hard to live by the precepts they heard on the Sabbath, and taught to their children.

The centurion took to heart the teachings he heard about charity and giving alms to the poor. He soon entered into the prayers and Scripture studies at the synagogue and his reputation as a godly man soon spread throughout the town.

There was one teaching that caused him to spend much time pondering it's meaning. The rabbi of the synagogue at Caesarea spoke a lot about the expectation of the coming of a Messiah, one sent from God to deliver the Jews from oppression. As a member of the Roman army Cornelius knew that he was considered by many to be one of the oppressors. But he did not feel that he was an enemy of these people. In fact he felt more like a protector. In his reading of the Scriptures Cornelius could not find a picture of a conquering hero. Rather it seemed to him that if a Messiah did appear he would come as a servant to the people. Cornelius saw the Messiah as one who would be concerned with souls of the people rather than their politics.

The centurion had found that he was not the only one to see a Messiah in that fashion. There were some Jews who felt that a Messiah may had already made his appearance in Judea. Some men from Jerusalem spoke of a man that the officials had executed and now the claim was made that he had come back from the dead. Cornelius found these claims to be fantastic but yet there was something about it that roused his curiosity.

One morning after they had eaten breakfast Cornelius' wife said to him, "What is bothering you today? I have never seen you so quiet. You have hardly spoken to me. Not even given the boys instructions about what they are to do today. And last night you barely touched your supper. Are you not feeling well?"

For a while Cornelius did not answer, then turning towards his wife he asked, "Did you ever see a vision or see a being that you thought was an angel?"

Before she could answer he went on, "Yesterday, about the ninth hour while I was in prayer I was approached by a man in shining clothes who said that he was a messenger from God."

"Cornelius, are you sure he was from God? Did he say that he was from God? And what did he say?"

"He said, dear wife, that God had heard my prayers and I should send for a certain Simon who would teach me more about God's will."

"But, where is this Simon? Is he here in Caesarea? If he is I have not heard of him."

"The man told me that Simon was staying with the tanner over in Joppa. I have thought of nothing else since this happened and I have decided that he was truly a messenger from God. If he was from God, and I really believe he was, then I must send for this Simon right away."

"What is it that Simon is supposed to teach you?"

"I have decided that it will be about the Galilean that the men from Jerusalem were talking about. The one that was executed and then rose from the dead. I want to hear more of that."

"Are you going to send for him now?"

"My delegation will be on the way by mid-day."

"Cornelius does this man know that you are not Jewish. You know how we Jews are about dealing with Gentiles."

The centurion could not help laughing. "My dear wife. You married a Gentile. What objection could he have to coming to see me. I do attend the synagogue you know."

"Yes I know that, but does he know that?"

"I think that God knows that and he is the one who had me send for Simon. If God spoke to me about this matter I think that maybe He has spoken to Simon also. We will see, we will see."

A New Partnership

Acts: 15: 36-41

"Silas my friend, welcome. Come in and rest for a while. I hear that you are planning to make a journey and visit the brothers in Syria and Cilicia."

The older man came into the dimly lit room and found a chair near the charcoal brazier and began to warm his hands.

"Peace to you brother Paul. I do need to rest for a while. We have walked all over Antioch this day, visiting our friends here before we leave on our journey to Syria. Our friends here are much encouraged by the letter from James which confirmed that the message of our Lord Jesus is for all, Gentile or Jew. I think that the work here will prosper even though some us will be gone for several months."

Paul rose and handed Silas a plate of bread and fish and a small bowl of wine.

"Take this Silas. I would wager that you have hardly eaten a thing this whole day. You must keep up your strength if you are to make the arduous journey you have planned. And my friend I think that a good idea would be for us to go together. As you know I have been in that region and have many friends there and I am familiar with many of the roads."

Silas looked up with a look of surprise, "I would like nothing better than to make this journey with you, my friend, but I thought that you were going to be traveling with Barnabas, perhaps back to Cyprus."

"That was the plan at one time, but Barnabas and I have had a disagreement over who should be in the traveling party. He would take John Mark with us again and I felt that it would not be the thing to do."

"Now Paul, I know that he is a young fellow but I think that he has a lot of potential. Don't you think that he would be a lot of help. Especially when it came to writing letters to the folks back here. He has a certain knack, you know, for writing. They say that he is fluent in both Greek and Aramaic."

Paul looked at his friend Silas and spoke earnestly, "It is not his writing ability nor his youth that I am concerned about. You know that when Barnabas and I took him with us last year he was ready to turn back by the time that we got to Pamphylia. You well know that when we are out there preaching the word of the Lord there are going to be hard and difficult times and if we turned back every time we ran into difficulty the Good News would never reach the people."

Silas nodded his head in agreement. "You speak the truth Paul. We must have courage and keep our head up when things become hard. But the only way we can learn how to face the evils of this world is to do it. I believe that John Mark will grow in strength and courage if we just give him time. You know, I think his problem last time was just a case of homesickness. And it just may be that having to leave when he was just getting to know that young daughter of Jairus' had something to do with it. We were all young once."

"Homesickness is no excuse for failure in the Lord's work. Home is where you are called to be. As for the girl; there comes a time when a man must decide between home and family and the call to spread the news about our risen Lord. I think that it will most difficult to have a wife and children and do what we are called to do. Silas you are married, what do you think?"

Silas replied, "I think that it can be very hard. My children are all grown and my wife has made her home with the oldest son for the past few years, when I have been gone so much. But if fifteen years ago you had asked me to do the work that I am now about, it would have been a hard decision. I think that the Holy One approves of a man taking good care of his family."

"Perhaps you are right my friend. But if a man does not marry then he does not have to be concerned about these things. Of course, every man is not called to do this work, but if you do then you must not give up, or turn back. The Lord will reward the faithful, the ones who fight the good fight. In any case, Barnabas has already made arrangements to sail for Cyprus by the end of the week and he will take John Mark with him. They go with my blessings."

Silas set down the wine bowl and looking Paul in the eye, he said, "Then it is set. We will work together and I am sure that the Holy One will bless our efforts. I look forward to spending this time with you and learning from you what you have heard directly from the Lord and the apostles. And Paul, I must say that I do not think that you have heard the last of the young fellow, John Mark. I think that one day he will be a mighty asset in the work."

Paul laughed, "Silas if you think so it may be so. We'll see; we'll see."

Demetrius, the Silversmith

Acts 19: 23-41

I don't remember exactly what year it was but it was right soon after that fellow Paul and his friends came to town. You remember Paul don't you? He was the one who went around talking about some man from over near Jerusalem. Claimed that the Romans had executed him and then a few days later came to life again. You would think that no one would put much stock in a crazy tale like that but they tell me that there are several people here in the city who claim to believe it. And furthermore, some of them say that this fellow who was supposed to be dead and is now alive will be showing up again around here one of these days.

Well, I can tell you when it was, close anyway. It was the last year that old man, Secundus, was the city clerk. In fact, it was him that jumped in and broke things up when we were about to get rid of that Paul and his followers for good.

You say you want to know about that riot that happened back then. I'll tell you all about it if you promise to keep your mouth shut about it. Those Romans have long memories about things like that.

Ephesus is a right good town don't you think. I have lived here most of my life and done pretty well for myself, if I do say so. Been in the silver business all of my life. When I was a young man I used to go up to the mines and buy the silver and bring it back here and sell to the artisans who make jewelry with it. After a time it got to be too much for me. Three hundred miles on a mule is strictly a young man's game; not to speak of the robbers and possible ship wreck if you took the sea route.

One day it came to me like a bolt out of the blue. I mean I had the best idea since the first man thought to milk a goat. It happened one day when I found I could hardly get through town for all the people who had come for a festival at the temple of the goddess Diana. Some of the silversmiths had told me that they did a fair business with some of those folks from out of town but they could only deal with the ones who were reasonably well off. I knew that we should come up with something that would sell to the masses.

Here is the idea I had. Why not make little statues of the goddess and sell them to the people so they could take them home and show off where they had been. I have to tell you that the idea do not go over with all the men in the guild at first. I remember one of them said to me, "Demetrius, you are crazy. I can think of two reasons that this will not work. If they have a silver idol that they can take home and worship then why would they want to come back to Ephesus. And secondly, I don't think that many of them could afford to buy a statue made of silver."

That ninny. I had to explain it all to him.

First of all. In my opinion, worship is not all these men have in mind when they go up to the temple. You know that there are dozens of temple prostitutes working there any time of the day or night; something that does not happen in the small villages that most of them come from. Second, who said that the little idols had to be made of pure silver. Not one in a thousand of them could tell if they were all silver or just had a thin plating. It was not long before most of the silversmiths saw the wisdom of my plan. And I am here to tell you that it worked like a charm.

Most of us did better at that than we ever did making bracelets and that sort of thing. I admit it was kind of seasonal but when we were not busy selling, we had time to do the manufacturing. A few of the men tried to cut corners too much when. it came to the silver and we had to straighten that out before it hurt business for all of us. But all in all it proved to be a profitable thing for most of the guild.

Now I am here to tell you that when you have a good thing going someone will try to horn in on it. On festival days some men from over at Corinth would sometimes come over here and try to sell Diana statues that they had made from marble, some of which they had dressed up with some precious stones. At least they claimed they were precious. I am here to tell you that we put a stop to that about the second time they showed up.

By the time they had to stagger home with knots on their heads they thought that coming to Ephesus was not too good for their health.

I guess that I am wandering a bit with this story but it all leads up to that incident you asked me about.

Things were going just fine when that fellow Paul showed up here. No, he was not selling anything in competition with us. In fact, he claimed to be a tent maker but I never saw him make a tent. What he was a trouble maker. Going around telling people that our Diana was no goddess at all. He was a Jew they say but he talked to the native folks as well as that bunch of Jews that have been here for many moons. I think that he was pushing a god of his own. Not really a god I don i t think but some man that the Romans killed and then it was claimed he came back to life in a few days, like I mentioned before.

At first, I did not worry too much about him, but you know, some people will fall for any cock and bull story. After a time, I heard that some folks were not buying from us because of what that little Jew was saying. We were not hurting yet, but that sort of thing has to be nipped in the bud. So, I had another of my brilliant ideas.

It was simple really. First, just sell the rest of the silversmith's guild on the idea that Paul was a threat to our living. That was not too hard. Some of them had heard him speak around town and were quick to agree with me that he was a threat to the worship of Diana. And they had seen how quick we were in getting rid of those interlopers from over at Corinth.

So one day a group of us set out to find this Paul and rough him up a bit. But finding him turned out to be harder than we thought. I think that some had never heard of him and others were protecting him by lying and saying that they didn't know him. It turned out that we found two fellows who turned out to be followers of his. They were a couple of foreigners from Macedonia. You know we ought to do something about letting all those people from other countries come in here if they are not here to worship our goddess, Diana.

But I digress. They had come here with that Paul, so we were obliged to teach them a lesson. One was called Gaius and the other Aristarchus. We grabbed them up and started over to the theatre with them and as they argued with us and we were telling them of the error of their ways I guess things got rather noisy. That drew a rather sizable crowd who followed along with us. Most of them did not know what it was all about. But you know how it is, a crowd draws a crowd and I was smart enough to make good use of them.

I jumped up in front of the crowd when we got to the theatre and harangued the crowd about the virtues of the worship of Diana and pointed out that these foreigners were subverting our special religion here in Ephesus. I had them pretty well worked up when a Jew named Alexander jumped up on the platform and tried to say that the two were innocent of subversion, but we shouted him downright quick. Then one of the younger guild members leaped up in front and began to shout, "Great is Diana of the Ephesians; Great is Diana of the Ephesians!" Almost immediately the crowd took it up and I'll take an oath, they kept it up for over two hours.

That's when that old bird, Secundus, showed up. Everybody knew him and when he stood up they got sort of quiet and they figured that the town clerk would tell what to do with those two foreigners. But the old buzzard fooled me. He started to tell how Ephesus was famous all over the world as the location of the great temple to Diana and we did not have any need to defend it. Then he said that if word of this ruckus got back to the Roman garrison the commander there would be very unhappy. He was charged to keep the peace and he would do it by persuasion or force, depending on his mood. If those Roman soldiers were called out Secundus said, we would all be unhappy.

It turned out it all came to naught. We had to turn the two Macedonians loose and never did find that Paul. The crowd just went into the taverns near the theatre and decided that a flagon of wine would go better than a Roman sword.

114

Since then I have heard that Paul has traveled all over the world telling about that God of his. In fact, I heard recently that he may by in Rome. Been arrested they say. I say that we will hear no more of him.

Remembering a Shipwreck

"An older man is at the front gate your excellency. He says that you are expecting him."

"Yes, yes, show him in, and fetch some refreshment also. I will meet him on the side porch where the shade is best."

Publius pulled himself to his feet and taking his cane moved towards the porch. He had been moving rather slowly for some time now but hoped that as the weather warmed he would be feeling better soon. Publius had been a Roman civil servant for a lifetime and now in his twilight years he had been assigned to the city of Rome where he had spent his boyhood years. Having served as governor for many years on the island of Malta he was now rewarded with a comfortable position near his old home on the outskirts of Rome.

Just as Publius found a seat on the porch his servant came out accompanied by a man of about his own age. Even though his guest was not dressed military garb Publius would have known at a glance that he was, or had been, a soldier. His hair was snow white, as was his beard, but his back was straight, and he walked with the assurance of a man that was used to being in charge.

"Greetings sir. Please be seated and forgive me if I do not rise. I just sat down and getting up has gotten to be rather a trial."

The old soldier found himself a chair and turned it to face his host. "Your excellency, you have a fine home here. I have passed it many times but never thought I would ever be inside. I confess that I was somewhat surprised when I received your invitation to visit."

Publius smiled as he replied, "I am afraid that I have been remiss in my hospitality of late. I have seen you in the village on occasion, with some children that I take to be your grandchildren, but it was only recently that I learned that we were acquaintances from many years back. Are you not Julius, and served in the Imperial Guard at one time?"

"Yes sir. You are right there but I cannot recall when we met. But, of course, I served for a lot a years and all over the empire and met many people. When do you think it was that we were acquainted?"

"Ah, Julius, I can understand why you do not remember me. It was about forty years ago on Malta. The ship you were on ran aground in a storm and broke up on the beach. I remember that you were in charge of a small detachment of men and you had at least one prisoner. Coming very close to drowning and having to see about your men and the ships passengers, it's no wonder that you do not remember every detail of that time."

Julius looked at his host and recognition came to his face. "Of course, now I know. You lived in the estate near the water and you and your people were very kind to us that day. Helped dry us out and fed us well. I remember that you helped us find another ship so that we eventually got to Rome. This is where we were headed on that trip. I made the

117

trip from the East end of the Great Sea to Rome several times. Escorting dignitaries and prisoners was one of my duties for several years. The voyage you refer to was one of the hardest I ever made. I thought more than once it would be my last one.

Publius leaned forward and said, "I take it that now like me you find the years catching up to you. and you are drawing your soldiers pension."

"My pension is a small piece of land near here that is my reward for fifty years' service to the Empire. I am not complaining you understand. Many soldiers have had to serve a lifetime in places a long way from their home and never got back there. In fact, things have worked out pretty well for me here. My first wife died several years ago while we were serving in a town called Caesarea, which you may be familiar with. After I was released from the Guard and came here I built a small house. Then it was my good fortune to marry the daughter of a cousin of mine. She is a bit younger than I but a good worker and respects her elders. We have two children and I have hopes that they will take care of me when I get past caring for myself. Oh, please pardon me for rambling on about myself. I'm sure you did not invite me here to hear about my family."

"Julius my friend, I am pleased to hear that you are doing so well. I think that a young family is just what a man needs to keep him on his toes. I take it that the little ones I saw with you were yours and not grandchildren as I supposed."

Julius smiled and nodded in agreement.

Publius called for the servant to bring some wine and cakes and after they had been served he said, "Julius the reason I wanted to talk to you was to find out if you remembered much about the prisoner you had with you on that day of the ship wreck. I know it has been a long time, but can you tell me anything about him? His name was Paul and he was from Jerusalem or at least from that area. The thing that impressed me at the time was his ability to heal the sick just by laying his hands on them. Since then I have heard more of the man and wondered what you knew of him. You were, after all with him for several weeks, were you not?"

"Yes, I was. And after all these years the memory of the man sticks in my mind. He was not the usual prisoner that I had to transport. Most of the time I would have to keep a close watch on a prisoner or they would try to escape. But not this man. As near as I could tell he was not a criminal. He had just got caught up in some kind of religious dispute between two groups of Jews. He was Jewish you know. I never did how just what the charge was but someone must have thought it was serious because he had appealed his case to Caesar. It was just my job to transport prisoners. Most of the tine I did not know the particulars of the case. What I remember about the man, Paul, was that he was totally unruffled about the whole thing. In fact I think that he was glad to be going to Rome. Sort of like it was his idea all along. And he had lots of friends. When we would make port he always knew someone there and they obviously thought well of him."

Publius leaned forward and asked, "Julius, did you ever hear Paul talk about his God or about a person called Jesus?"

Julius thought for a minute and then said, "I cannot remember his exact words but on maybe two occasions when the weather was really rough and most of us were afraid we would not make it Paul said that it had been revealed to him that none of us would perish. And it turned out that he was right. No body did drown although it was a very close call, as you know."

"Tell me, your Excellency, why after all the years has the subject of this man Paul come up? Surely it has nothing to do with the loss of the ship after all these years. I would wager that the man, Paul, is no longer alive. If he is he would be a hundred years old by now."

Publius replied, "My interest in the man is purely personal. Nothing official, I can assure you. Several years passed after the incident of the wreck before I again heard of Paul."

Publius leaned back in his chair and looked as if he was seeing something far away. "Julius, my life has changed since I came back here. More than just a new position. It's a whole new way of looking at things; a new way of believing how life should be lived."

"And I take it," Julius replied, "that this man Paul, must have had something to do with this change in your life."

"You are correct, and strangely enough, I never met the man after that incident forty years ago. At that time I knew very little of him and nothing of the work that he was doing. But since then I have heard much about him and indirectly his teachings have changed my life."

"His teaching you say. I thought that he was a scholar. I saw that he spoke several tongues and he was a writer also. I have always admired people with that talent. I never had any schooling myself, going into the army when I was not much more than a boy. After I attained the rank of officer I had, for many years, a slave from Alexandria who was an excellent scribe. Tell me, what was it that you learned of his teaching that changed your life, if that is not too personal?"

"It is very personal, Julius but I am glad for the opportunity to share it with you. When I arrived back in Rome I was assigned the duty of overseeing the inspection of things shipped into the country from foreign countries. To tell the truth it was more honorary that an actual job. But it was an excuse for my salary and I enjoyed meeting a lot of the travelers for many lands. I had not been at it very long before I met a couple who were originally from Pontus, a small town in Macedonia. His name was Aquila and his wife was Priscilla. They were returning to the city after being gone for several years. These folks had been forced to leave Rome when Claudius was Caesar. They were Jews and you will remember that Claudius did not like that race. In fact he had most of them run out of Rome during his tenure on the throne."

Julius looked serious as he replied, "I have heard something of what you say but to tell you the truth, one reason that I had a long career on the military was that I kept a deaf ear to the politics of Rome and what I did hear I did not repeat."

"You are wise man Julius. But knowing which way the wind was blowing is what kept me in office for all these years. We may now speak of Claudius since it has been enough years that all his friends have followed him to their final destination. But we are not here to speak ill of the dead. It was just an explanation of how my friends happened to be away from the city for years. They became my dearest and closest friends. Aquila died a few ago and Priscilla is rather infirm but still of quick mind. She now makes her home here with us."

"Your Excellency, I do not think that you are a Jew, but it seems that you have or have had several Jewish friends. Have you decided to become one of them? Is that the life change that you spoke of?"

"Julius, have you heard of the movement called The Way or sometimes called Christians?"

"Yes I have. Though I do not know much about them. My wife has said that she has met some of them at the market and tells me that they are mostly common folk but they are always nice to her. She has heard stories that they have some very unusual rituals, such as eating bread and calling it the flesh of a martyred hero of theirs. Was this fellow Paul one of that group do you think?"

"Paul was very much one of them and much of what they believe, and practice comes from his teachings and writings. But Paul was only a messenger who taught about The Way. The central figure in this movement is a man called Jesus, a Jew from the territory of Galilee, a few miles north of Jerusalem. I have become very much interested in The Way, or Christianity, as it is now being called. That is why I wanted to know if you could tell me more about this man Paul. His writings about Jesus and the way believers should live have wrought a great change in me. I have learned much from Priscilla and Aquila. They were believers in Christianity from the very early days and I have to tell- you that I now am a believer and I try to learn more about Jesus and his teaching every way I can."

Julius leaned back in his chair and thought a minute before saying, "Does this mean that you have forsaken the traditional gods of the Romans?"

"Yes, it does, except that I never did put much stock in the gods that we have heard about all our lives. I always took it as just stories made up for our amusement. What we believed about those gods did not effect how we lived or how we died for that matter. I have now found the true God who cares for his people and wants us to live a richer and happier life."

"Is this Jesus that Paul writes of; is he the God that you now follow and perhaps worship?"

"Yes Julius. Jesus was God sent into the world by the Father God. You might say that he is the Son of God. He came to man preaching that we are to love one another and to love God. Further he said that we could be forgiven of the wicked and wrong things that we have done in our lifetime. The ritual that you spoke of, the eating of the bread. We do that to remind us that Jesus not only lived but died and then came back to life and one day he will return to his people and many more will believe in him, just like I do now."

Julius sat silent a time. before saying, "I have seen enough of the wickedness of the world to see that we need more love and certainly some of us would like to know that we are no longer being blamed for past mistakes. But I also know that forgiveness is a rare commodity in this world. Revenge and punishment are more common in the world that I have lived most of my life in."

With a smile Publius said, "You are absolutely right. That is why the message of our Lord Jesus is so vital. Since the first man trod this old earth revenge has been more common than forgiveness; hate more common than love, and ambition more common than humility. Julius, if everyone would live by the teachings of Jesus there would be no need of soldiers. But I know that it will never happen. I just know that if I will live like He taught then I, and a few more, will live a happier life. You know one of the things Jesus said was,

"Do to people like you want them to do to you." What do you think of that?"

Julius laughed and replied, "I think that if I had lived like that as a soldier some pagan would have run me through with a sword a long time ago. Keep your guard up and strike first if you want to live to be an old soldier."

"Ah, wisdom of the world Julius. And all it has gotten us is war, hate, revenge and much misery. I mentioned that I have been reading some of the writings of Paul. In a letter that he wrote to the Christians at Corinth he said that we must have "Faith, Hope and Love and the greatest of these is Love. Faith in the teachings Of Jesus, a Hope that they will prevail in the world and he said that love is the greatest of all." It is also the teaching of The Way that we are to help the poor and the ill and the widow and the orphan. Surely no one could say that that is not a valuable teaching. Further, our Lord Jesus taught that if we are faithful that there will be a reward for us after we have died. On the last night before he died he said…"

"Wait now," Julius interrupted. "Did you say a reward after you die. I think that this is getting a little too strange for an old soldier."

"Julius, didn't you say that you remember how Paul seemed to be so calm and sure even when it looked like death might be imminent? One time near the end of his life he wrote to a friend, "I have fought the good fight, I have finished the race, I have kept the faith. Now there is in store for me the crown of righteousness, which the Lord, the righteous judge, will award to me on that day." You see, Paul knew that a reward awaited him and all who are faithful to the teachings of the Lord Jesus."

As Julius got to his feet he said, "I must be going now but I am ready to hear more about this Jesus and the writings of the man Paul. When do think that we may talk again?"

"'Come back on the first day of the week. A group will be here, and we always speak of these things. I am sure that you will be enlightened."

"Thank you, your Excellency, I will see you then."

Two Friends in the Faith

"Eutychus, oh Eutychus. Is that really you?"

The young man turned, saw who was calling his name and with a big smile called out, "Trohimus, my friend, it surely is me, and what a treat to see you here in Rome, of all places. What brings you here to this den of idol worshipers?"

As the two men embraced, Trohimus said, " I was about to ask you the same thing. The last I heard you were still in Jerusalem."

Eutychus took his friend by the arm and led him to side of the road. "Let's get over here out of the hot sun where we can sit in the shade and I can tell you about my travels and how I came to be here."

Finding a stone bench in the shade of a tall olive tree the two sat down, each eager to catch up on what was happening in the life of the other.

"Trohimus, I'm sure that you remember that I was always a part of the church in Jerusalem, from the time I was just a boy. I have been acquainted with the Master's chosen twelve and have sat at the feet of our esteemed leader, Paul, for these many years."

Trohimus smiled and replied, "Of course I remember, you have been a notable part of the Way since before I came to find my way into the grace of the Lord.   And I have heard many times how Brother Paul laid hands on you,

126

reviving you when you were taken for dead after your terrible fall. And I have heard how you happen to take that fall." This was said with a twinkle in his eye and a laugh that can be found between old friends.

Eutychus joined in the laughter. "Oh, that story has been told a hundred times, but I don't mind. My going to sleep and falling from a window during a worship service was just an opportunity to show the power of the spirit that was and still is working though Brother Paul. And I was just a boy at the time. That can be my excuse. But you asked how I came to be in Rome. Well, I have been here for a few years now, having come when Paul asked me to bring a letter he had written to the new church here. We were at Corinth when he wrote to them. The plan, I think, was to go to Jerusalem then from there on to Rome. The church here was rather new at the time and Brother Paul felt like they needed some instruction in living the righteous life, so after bringing the letter I felt called to stay and be of what help I could. Many a time I have suffered from what some call home sickness, but I guess that this is the place that the Lord would have me work. You know Paul did get to Rome but not in the way that he planned. As someone said, "The Lord works in mysterious ways." In fact, he is here now, having recently arrived and I have not been able to see him yet because I was down at Petioli where a small group of the brethren have begun to meet and worship in the house of the mayor there. I was on the way into town to meet him when you called out to me. Did you know that he arrived here as a prisoner? I'm not sure about that but I heard that just this morning."

"Eutychus, you can be sure that you heard right. I am here in Rome because I booked passage on the same boat that brought Brother Paul here. When you see him you will find out that I was part of the reason that he was arrested. I felt obligated to come along with him and be of what help I could."

"But Trohimus, how could you be blamed for anything that he did. I realize, of course that those in Jerusalem would use any excuse to persecute Paul but you haven't spent much time in the Holy City. In fact I thought you were living in Ephesus."

"You are right, I am from Ephesus and was one of the first non-Hebrews there to come to believe in Jesus Christ, but I accompanied Paul to Jerusalem when we delivered the alms given to the poor in that city that Paul had collected from other churches. It turned out that I was seen in the city with Paul and some radical Jews thought Paul had taken me into the temple with him, and you well know that they would think that I would desecrate they temple. I could debate that question all day but we both know the laws about that. Brother Paul was attacked by a wild mob and could well have been killed if the Roman soldiers had not intervened quickly. Being a Roman citizen was what got him a fair hearing before two governors and King Agrippa. Even though these men of authority found no reason to punish Paul they did yield to the pressure from the local religious leaders and so Brother Paul finds himself here to be heard by Caesar: The man has suffered much doing what he was called to do; spread the good news of the Gospel of Jesus Christ. And he says that this latest trial and imprisonment may be God's way of getting him to Rome, where he has wanted to come for years. I just do not know what to think about this hearing he is to have with Caesar. He has done nothing amiss according to Roman law but you can never know what heathen rulers might do. And you will be pleased to know that our good friend Doctor Luke came to Rome with us."

Eutychus got to his feet and said, "Let's be going along as we talk. I am anxious to see Brother Paul. It has been a few years since I left him back in Ephesus. He has always been like a father to me you know; and to a lot of others I suspect. I was thinking that when his hearing comes up we could be there to vouch for his good character and witness to the fact that he has always obeyed the Roman law and in fact, is proud to be a Roman citizen."

"I agree with you on that my friend, but there is one thing that worries me. I have heard talk that the emperor may declare himself a god and the people will be compelled to worship him. You well know that Paul, or any believer for that matter, will not worship or pray to any heathen ruler. If this comes about I can see that Brother Paul could be in real danger."

Eutychus frowned as he considered that last thought, then said, "I can see where the followers of the Way might have much trouble if that comes about, but not only them but also the Jews who live under Roman rule, and there are many of us. And oh, I am looking forward to seeing the good doctor again, and I know that Brother Paul appreciates having Luke with him. Having lived a hard life, it must be good to have the man of medicine near at hand."

Trohimus nodded in agreement. "Another thing that Luke is doing is to write down how things are going and a history of the churches where the Way has begun. He is a friend of Brother Peter and has learned much of the very early days of the movement, as well as traveling many miles with Paul. I believe that the generations that follow us will be interested to know these things; that is if the Lord has not returned before then."

As the two rounded a corner they could see the house where Paul was being held, and Eutychus hurried on ahead and was astounded to see a crowd of men around the front of the house. Looking back at Trohimus he asked, "What do you think has happened? Has there been some trouble do you think?"

"No trouble my friend, just Paul doing what he always does. He has invited the local Jews to come visit with him. You know that he never misses an opportunity to speak a word for our Christ Jesus. A prisoner, a teacher, a faithful witness to everything that he has seen and heard and believes. Let us go in my friend. I am sure that we still have much to learn."

Hospitality

"Joine, I am surprised at you. You have always been willing to be gracious to all who come to our home, and now, look at you, throwing a fit just because I mentioned inviting some travelers in for a meal and a time of rest." As he spoke the man paced the floor of the small kitchen and frowned at his wife who stood, hands on hips, next to a small table.

"Well Zanen, I don't know why you are surprised. You have heard the same thing that I have about those men. The one they call Paul has stirred up trouble in towns North of here and you want him to be welcome in this house? This morning while I was at the well…"

"Yes, yes, I can imagine what you might hear down there from those ladies who never laid eyes on the man Paul but claim to know all about him. What I have heard is that he is an educated teacher who has some strong, and maybe new, ideas about how we are to know the Holy One."

The woman sat down on the bench behind the table and said, "Don't we have the Law and the Prophets to tell us all we know about the Almighty? Why would we want to listen to a man like that? Maria told me that her husband was at the synagogue at his brother's village last sabbath and that man Paul was asked to read the scripture, which he did, then he began to speak about the coming of the Messiah, and claimed that he, Paul, had even met the Messiah. Now tell me if that sounds sensible to you."

Zanen waked over to the door and stood looking out at the dusty street and thought a while before he spoke. "What we know about the Holy One does not always seem sensible or practical. Sometimes there must be a bit of faith woven into we believe about such matters. I would like to hear what the man has to say, I might learn something from him."

The wife began to knead some dough as she replied, "Maria told me that there are at least three men in that group. One of them, she says, is said to be a doctor who is always writing about no telling what. And the other is an older man called Silas who also does some teaching, or at least he talks a lot. Maria's husband says that in some towns where they go, they even invite women join in discussions about spiritual things. Now what do you think of that?"

Zanen smiled as he said, "I think that Maria knows more about them than anybody in the town. She may want to talk to them herself if it is true about women being welcome in their discussions, not in the synagogue of course. Now wife, do you think you could welcome them here for a meal this evening, and perhaps for a night's rest?"

"I suppose so. Now go fetch me some more flour. I'll have to bake while you talk."

Profit

"Wait Joram, let me hold his head while you get the pack off." The two men were wrestling with a recalcitrant donkey who did not want to be handled. With one at the head and the other unfastening the girth the sack of barley was dropped to the ground and a large jar of oil was lifted off without further trouble.

"Thank you, neighbor, you came along just when help was needed. And, by the way, would you like to buy a big stout ass?"

The neighbor, Elah, laughed, "Big and strong is right. What about well trained and tame to handle? You will have a hard time selling that beast around here; we all know him too well. But I did not come by just to hold stubborn donkeys. I knew you were in the village yesterday and was wondering if you saw the rabbi, Jesus. I heard that he was in the area."

Joram took a seat on a low stone wall as he said, "Yes I saw him and stayed around a while to hear what he had to say. But I am here to tell you, I just don't know what to make of it."

Elah handed the donkey's lead to Joram, then sat down beside him on the wall. "Tell me friend, what did Jesus talk about. I wanted to be there myself, but, you know how the wife has been lately, and I just could not leave the house."

Joram thought for a minute then said, "He told a story about a rich ruler who gave a lot of gold to three of his workers and expected them to take it and make a lot of profit from it while he, the ruler, was gone away for some time. The rich man then generously rewarded the ones who were successful in their business ventures with the gold. And he severely punished the servant who failed to make any profit. I am sure that there was supposed to be a lesson learned from that story but just what it is, I am not sure. My impression of the Teacher is of one that is not too concerned with profit or having a lot of property. Now listening to him, it sounded like old Abe the fish dealer, fussing at his son for not charging enough."

"You are correct," said Elah, "that does not sound like the Teacher. Maybe he was using the rich ruler as an example of how most of our earthly rulers, or Caesars are. But they say that he never gets into politics either."

"No, he was not talking about any rich business man or king, I don't think. He was saying that about the Kingdom of Heaven. Now does that make any sense to you?"

"Oh, maybe I am beginning see something here, replied Elah. If he was talking about a Godly kingdom, then perhaps he was speaking about heavenly gold; or things that we own that are not temporal but eternal. Things like honesty, faith, and such things. I can see that Jesus would want us to multiply these attributes. Good works and charity might be included in this list. And not using them would bring about God's displeasure, maybe even punishment. I need to hear more about this."

Amittai

"Greetings Amittai. How are things with you this fine morning?"

"About as well as could be expected", the older gentlemen replied. "A man of my age should not be out here looking for lost goats, but here I am. And you Jabed, are you feeling better than you were when we last met?"

"Yes, the fever seems to have left me and feel like a young buck of a man now. I am in no hurry to get back to the house, so let me help you locate those wayward goats."

Even with a difference in ages the two men had been friends for many years and were comfortable in their discussions; whether it be family, religion, or their thoughts on the latest ruler.

They agreed that climbing to the top of a near ridge would give them a good view of the terrain there abouts and maybe they could spot the runaways. By the time they got to the crest of the hill they were both out of breath and Jabed suggested that they sit down for a spell. Finding a flat top rock about knee high they took a rest and Amittai worked a pebble from his sandal as Jabed said, "I was talking to some of the ladies down by the well yesterday, and they telling me that Jonah is back home and I was surprised because I have not seen him. It's his habit to be where the men tend to gather and to speak about what he deems to be the will of the Most High."

With a deep breath, Amittai replied, "Yes, he is back after many months when we did not know where he was. You will remember that when he left he told us that he was going to Spain. And I confess I do not know where a place is called Spain and he was never clear about why he should go there. As you said Jabed, Jonah felt that he was catled by our God to help us know the will of our Maker; he still feels that way but since his return he seems uneasy about his calling as a prophet. And I think that he really is a man called by the Most High, but since his return he has kept mostly to himself and spends a lot of times just thinking, or as he would say, meditating. That's why you haven't seen him. Mostly he stays out with the sheep and the goats and I guess he was meditating, or napping, when three of them wandered off. I do not know where he is this morning so here I am out here goat looking."

Getting to his feet, Jabed pointed down toward a small stream in the valley below them. "I believe I see your goats lying in that grassy spot near that big tree. We should be able to get them headed toward home without too much trouble."

And the two men did just that. Experienced in that sort of thing they soon had the animals back with the flock, Amittia laid a hand on Jabed's shoulder and said, "Many thanks, my friend. A good neighbor like you is worth more than gold. Now I wonder where Jonah is this morning. I would like for you to see him. Maybe he would tell you what it is that seems to have him so troubled since returning from his trip to Spain. Jabed, do you know anything about this Spain?"

Stroking his beard Jabed said, "I have heard of it being at the far end of the great sea, many leagues from here. But why would Jonah want to go there. I hear that it is a land of heathens. Maybe he felt like he should go and tell them about the true God that we know. Has he not told you what he did there? Anyone else who had made that trip would be talking of nothing else."

Amittai shook his head and replied, "He has not said a word about Spain and strangely he has mentioned something about the city of Nineveh and the people there. If he was looking for heathens to preach too he would not have to go all the way to Spain. Plenty of heathens could be found in Nineveh."

It is interesting that he should speak of Nineveh, said Jabed. Just yesterday a wool buyer was in the area and he said that he had been in Nineveh recently and he noticed a change in the place. Not that the buildings were different, and they had the same old king, but he said it was the way the people acted. You know it has always been said that those folks over in Nineveh were hard to deal with; would cheat their grandmother for an extra drachma. Now, the wool man said, they would go out of their way to take a fair price for their wool. He was puzzled by all that but pleased of course. Do you think that Jonah has heard about what has happened in Nineveh and he might be interested, because he has always taught that knowing God's will affects the way we live?"

"Jabed, I doubt that Jonah would have any interest in what goes on in Nineveh. I have heard him speak of the place in very unflattering terms. In fact, he speaks of the place with hate in his voice. A tone that is not becoming to a man who is trying to be God's man in this world. The only thing he has really talked about was a time he was ship wrecked and was nearly drowned. Maybe he never did get to Spain because of that, and you know that he was never able to swim, but he told his mother about spending time in the ocean. How he got out alive he has never said."

"Well Amittai, I'm sure Jonah has respect for his father and if you would insist he would tell all that happened to him. There must be an interesting story there."

John Mark

I have lived here in this town of Antioch for several years now, and I am here to tell you that there is no more cantankerous place in all the empire. The Romans must keep a detachment of soldiers stationed here to keep the peace. There is always somebody raising a fuss about something. Taxes are the favorite target of their ire. And whoever is appointed town clerk is always accused of siding with the Romans or dipping into the town funds.

The old fellow who has the tax booth at the South Gate must be fattening his purse. He has married off two daughters with dowries that were the talk of the town. But, the biggest crook of them all is the one who is supposed to care for the water viaduct that we worked so hard to build back when I was a very young man. When a tall palm tree fell on it and caused a small leak, he required the ones living closes to it to pay for repairs. He collected from twice as many as was needed, then he built a new room on to his house. Those Roman soldiers backed him on this thing; so, I think they must have gotten a kick back too.

I will admit that there is one group in town that tries to live a quiet life, and they go out of their way to be a help to their neighbors. They have become known as The Way, and it seems that they have an informal organization. I don't know if their leaders are elected or I they are just recognized as qualified and step into that position. I do know that charity is an important to them, and they take care of their own group and they step out to help others. Further, they make an ongoing effort to reach out to other cities to enlist new members into their group. Growing the organization (The Way) seems to be the thing that take the biggest part of their time and resources. They are connected to other groups of The Way in other cities and I have heard that they send money to the other organizations if they are poor.

I am not an expert on these things, but I have been told that becoming a member of The Way is a matter of changing the way you live and what you believe about the gods. I do know that they have forsaken the traditional Greek and Roman gods and teach about the one God that the Hebrews have followed for many generations. I heard one of their number insist that their belief is in the Son of that God and further, that Son teaches that we must love that God and our fellow man as well. I have a hard time believing that these hardheaded citizens of Antioch could give any serious thought to loving the rest of us. Further, they say that this Son of Their God was arrested and executed by the Romans. When I heard about that I could not understand how people could be persuaded to join that organization, but I was still impressed by the life I saw them living.

The wife says that I am too curious and quick to look into things like this, but when I asked a few questions I found that the members of The Way were anxious to tell about what they believed. I think I will be talking to some of them again soon.

A man named Paul has been very influential in the group and I was hoping to talk with him, but I hear that he has just left for a trip across the Great Sea. He will probably be gone for months or maybe years. One of the younger members of The Way, (John Mark) was hoping to go with Paul and a fellow called Barnabas, but they wouldn't let him accompany them because of some disagreement they had had. They say that Paul is a pretty tough old bird and he expects others to be the same. It could be that a long trip with him could be a hard one, and I hear that he is going to try to make more converts to The Way. I don't know if he can do very well at that. We may have heard the last of him.

Jesus and Legion

"Lucas, do you really expect us to believe a story like that? I think that you have been too free with that wine your uncle makes."

There was laughter from the group of men gathered around a young man who was trying to get his breath and relate a strange story that his friends were slow to believe.

"I have known old Joram all my life," spoke up one of the men, "and he would never let anything like that happen to his hogs. He is far too stingy for that."

"I'll swear I saw it happen," replied Lucas. "That whole herd of pigs just ran down a steep hill and straight into the water. And nobody was chasing them either; just as if they all decided to drown themselves all at the same time."

"There must have been something going on to cause it to happen. Were there any strangers around that might have spooked them," asked one of the men.

Lucas nodded and said, "Yes, there were several people there on the hill above the lake. There was a teacher or priest or something like that over there, and there were several people who were following him. And others seemed to be there just to see him, or maybe to hear him teach."

One in the group spoke up, "That is an unusual place to be teaching. That is right next to the graveyard where that mad-man stays. You know, the one who calls himself Legion.

142

And old Joram's hogs run all over that hillside. Where do you think that teacher and his followers came from? Do you know?"

"You know Asa. He said that they came across the lake in a boat."

"Well, that tells us what caused the hogs to drown. I don't know how they did it, but they made it happen," said one of the group.

"What makes you so sure of that?" one of the men asked.

"If they came from the other side of the lake, they must be Hebrews, and we all know what they think of hogs. It would be just like them to want to do away with as many as they could."

"I'll tell you what else the teacher did. He talked to that crazy in the graveyard and suddenly the man looked like he was cured of what some call evil spirits. The two had a conversation like two men in their right mind. Asa said that the man, Legion he calls himself, started walking toward town telling everyone he met how the teacher had cured him."

After hearing Lucas's story, the men agreed that the teacher must be a man of amazing abilities, but they were sure that Joram would be sending him a bill for the hogs.

Made in the USA
Columbia, SC
15 June 2019